The Plan

A Breakbattle Academy Novel

Ruby Vincent

Published by Ruby Vincent, 2019.

Chapter One

"What the hell is this?!"

"Language, Jordan." Aunt Bev's bat ears picked her up from the hall. The clomp of her work boots reverberated off the walls, preceding her until she appeared in the doorway. "You don't need to— Hera, help me. What the hell is this?"

Disappointment settled in me and I swallowed hard around the lump in my throat. I should have known my family wouldn't sugarcoat things for me. That's not what the Manning women did.

"It's a disgrace is what it is." Mom pinched the pillow between two fingers and held it before her wrinkled nose. "There are stains on this! It looks as though they found this furniture on the side of the road."

Yep, no sugarcoating.

Mom turned away from the bed and flung the pillow in the direction of the waste bin. "I will buy you another one."

Jordan pushed past me into the room. "Might want to get her a mattress too... and a bed frame... and a new room."

I wished there was something I could say in defense of my dorm, but it was even more horrible than I imagined. A month ago, I slept in the A Class dorm on a bed that cradled me in a memory foam cocoon as I slept. I had a sitting area, television, my own desk, and a wardrobe.

If I hadn't passed through the gates and read Breakbattle Academy proudly emblazoned on the iron, I would have thought I entered a nightmare instead of my school for the next four years. There were no desks in here. There was no television. There was no sitting area. There weren't even chairs.

The only thing that greeted us in this minuscule space other than the bare metal-framed twin beds and the wooden trunks that lay before them, were the cracks in the plaster walls and the dust coating the single ceiling fan.

Aunt Bev let my duffel bag slip through her fingers as she planted her hands on her hips. "This is enough. You can't let her stay here, Brenda."

"My name is not—"

"Never mind that now," she snapped. "Are you seeing this? There are prison cells with more amenities!"

Jordan cringed. "Plus, no bathroom. I hate to say it, cuz, but maybe Mom is right. How is this supposed to work?"

I glanced at my mother and noted the slight frown as she looked around. This wasn't good. She couldn't change her mind now. Not when I was so close.

"I knew I wouldn't have a bathroom," I spoke up. "Only B Class and up get their own bathrooms while the rest of us have to use the showers on our floors. It's simple. I'll go early in the morning or late at night when they're still in bed."

Aunt Bev shook her head. "It would only take one night owl or early riser to stumble in and this will all go up in flames."

She had a point, but I wouldn't let on. "It's going to be fine, Auntie. Mom and I have already discussed it. Right?" I glanced at Mom who was still frowning. "Right, Mom?"

"Yes, we did," she said through pinched lips, "but this is worse than I was expecting."

My throat tightened. "What does that mean?"

"It means we'll need to give this space some upgrades if my child is supposed to stay here." She clicked her tongue. "We lived in villages with no plumbing or electricity and I'd take that over this. It's a disgrace and you can be sure I'll be putting it in the book. I can only imagine what it's like on the girl side."

Mom snagged Jordan's hand and pulled her toward the door. "Come with me. We're going shopping."

Jordan winked at me on the way out. "Don't worry. We'll turn this trash heap into something semi-livable."

I was so relieved Mom wasn't forcing me to leave all I could do was smile—that was until I turned and caught sight of Aunt Bev's piercing look.

"What's wrong?" I asked.

"I wonder if you've really thought this through—"

"I have."

"—because fooling a few boys for a week while they were focused on their tests and trials is very different from spending the next four years eating, living, and learning together. Not to mention, if you make real friends, your deception might eat away at you."

I tensed as her speech went on. "I know it won't be easy to keep my secret, but Mom and I discussed every possibility. Besides, they already think I'm a guy. Short of seeing me topless—which isn't going to happen—there's no reason for them to suspect I'm not."

She closed the distance between us. "And my last point about the guilt of lying to your friends and pretending to be someone you're not? What about that?"

My fists balled within the sleeves of my sweater. "It will be hard, but I have to do this."

"Why?" She looked hard at me, capturing my gaze and refusing to let go. "Why do you have to do this?"

"Mom's book—"

Aunt Bev held up a finger. "I told you I wouldn't hear that lie anymore. I know this is not about any book."

I pressed my lips together, falling silent. I couldn't tell her.

I could trust Jordan to keep my secret. I could trust Jordan with anything, but if I told Aunt Bev, she'd go straight to Mom no matter how much they fight. There was just no way she'd hide something like that from her sister and Mom would yank me out of this school the second she knew the truth. She might even yank me out of the country and take us back on the road. I wouldn't let that happen. Now that I was here, I was getting close to Derek Grayson. This was all about Derek.

We locked in a staredown that was only broken by the sound of voices in the hall. I blinked when I recognized them.

"—this room on the end."

"But damn this place is grim," said an older, deeper voice. "Worse than I remember. I'm pretty sure that skid mark on the wall has been there for the last twelve years."

"Jaxson," hissed a feminine voice. "Let's be more positive, please."

"It's okay, Mom," Adam replied as he pushed in the door. "I figured this was what I was in for when I got my placement."

Despite myself, and Aunt Beverly's watchful eye, a grin broke out on my face. "Adam! I can't believe it. We're roommates again?"

"Yep. I think Argyle felt bad about"—he gestured around us—"this, so she put us in the same room."

"We did say we'll be in this together," I said as he tromped inside weighted down with duffel bags. "At least until we can figure a way out of this mess."

Miss Val was right behind him. "I have spent the summer looking into that," she said. "You cannot retake the placement test, but you have the same chance to move up a class as the other students. So don't worry." She placed a hand on my shoulder. "Hard work does not go unnoticed at Breakbattle Academy."

"Thank you, Miss Val, I'm sure everything... will be... fine." My eyes drifted over her shoulder as the rest of Adam's party filed in.

Holy mother. Are they Adam's dads?!

One by one, the most gorgeous men I had ever seen out of a magazine, walked into our dingy room.

Miss Val looked over her shoulder. "Oh, Zeke. Let me introduce you to Adam's dads. This is Ezra."

A man with perfectly coiffed hair and striking dark eyes inclined his head as he set one of Adam's bags on the floor.

"This is Maverick."

My eyes went up, up, and up to peer at the massive hulk of smoldering muscle that waved to me.

"This is Ryder."

"Nice to meet you, Zeke." Ryder was next to shake my hand. The act brought him close enough that I could trace the edges of his raven-colored beard and wonder if I was truly look-ing into silver eyes.

"And this is—"

"Jaxson Van Zandt," said a blond man in a slick leather jacket and an even slicker grin. "The man. The legend." Jaxson sidled up behind Miss Val and wrapped his arms around her swelling abdomen. "You'll watch out for our firstborn, won't you?"

I cut eyes to Adam who was fighting a laugh. "I'll try, but I think it's him who'll be watching out for me. I only survived orientation week because of him."

Aunt Bev came up to me and put her arm around my shoulder. "Zeke was homeschooled up to now. This is his first year in a traditional school."

Jaxson whistled. "What a place to start out. Breakbattle is as far from traditional as it gets."

"Yes, I admit I had some reservations. I hoped my nephew would go to the local high school with my daughter, but he and his mother thought this place would be a better... fit."

Miss Val nodded, the pleasant smile still on her face. "I completely understand. No one wants to hear 'your child' and 'battle' in the same sentence. This school is built on ideas that many find radical."

"I'm worried about the toll this will take on him."

"I am too. Zeke's well-being is my top concern along with all of the students."

"Is it?"

"Yes, I'm the school therapist."

"You are?" I picked up a note of interest in her tone. "Will you be meeting with Zeke?"

"Twice a semester."

"I didn't know that." Aunt Bev shuttled me off to the side as she faced Miss Val. "Is it possible you two could meet more often?"

My eyes widened. "Aunt Bev?"

She went on like she didn't hear me. "Just with the home-schooling, flunking the placement test due to a vicious prank, and being surrounded by male peers for the first time, I think he may need more help adjusting."

"Aunt Bev!" I hissed.

She flapped a hand at me without looking my way. "Zeke, go help Adam unpack."

"Actually, we'll take over from here," Maverick spoke up. "Why don't you guys go find your friends?"

"Thanks, Dad. Owen and Justin just texted me that they were here. We'll go check out their rooms." Adam came over and grabbed my arm before I could protest. "Don't leave without saying goodbye, okay?"

Ryder leaned over and ruffled Adam's curls. "We won't, son."

"I'm definitely open for more sessions for students who need them," Miss Val said as Adam dragged me out. "But Zeke's mom would have to request them."

"I'm sure my sister will agree with me that..."

My stomach was a tangle of knots as we left our new dorm behind. I did not like where that conversation was going. Aunt Beverly was being good about using "he," "Zeke," and "nephew," but it would only take one slipup to sink me.

"You mad about being in the F Class?"

Adam's voice brought me out of my thoughts. I glanced over at him as we headed for the stairwell.

The hallway was empty except for us. I came early to lessen the shock for my family of seeing a parade of boys stomping in and out of my new home, and no doubt Adam did the same because his mother had to report for work. Something about this felt like peace before the storm and I wanted to enjoy it before everyone else came—before the Elite arrived.

"No, I'm not," I said honestly. "I'm just happy to be here. That stunt Cam and his buddies pulled could have gotten our admission rejected."

He scoffed. "I have no doubt that was the idea. I've been thinking about it all summer and it was planned. Santi getting us out of the cafeteria when he did. Cam stalling us until he dropped the final ultimatum. If we had agreed, we would have made it to the test with the other guys, but running to get help would have doomed anyone to miss it and get kicked out of the Elites and Breakbattle. We were only saved because Mom fought for us."

"Their plan was exceptionally cruel and devious."

Adam gave me a look as we reached the third-floor landing. "You've summed up Cameron Dupre perfectly. Exceptionally cruel and devious."

There was nothing to say in response to that. Every orientation the Elites came up with something to test the newbies, but it was Cameron's idea to *murder* Derek. What kind of sixteen-year-old would come up with a test so twisted?

My mind didn't offer up an answer to that question so I tried not to think about it. There was plenty of time to worry about Cameron and the rest of the Elite Network.

It was Sunday and move-in day. After unpacking and saying goodbye to our families, we would meet up in the auditorium where the battle system and life at our new school would be explained. Then the next day would be the first day of classes and the official start of the year. I was being thrown right in and even though I had no doubt I hadn't heard the last of the Elite Network, I needed to focus on the real reason I was here.

"Owen is in the room on the end," Adam said. "399."

I glanced around the hall, taking in the stark differences from the one I had just left. The C hall wasn't on the same level as the A hall, but there were no skids on these walls. The wallpaper was a clean simple cream and the gray carpets were stain-free.

"I'm glad he got into the C Class," I said. "Showing up to orientation with a broken arm was the worst luck, but he got through."

"I think he would have been in the A Class if his scores on the trials hadn't brought him down. I wish they'd bend on their 'no exceptions' rule."

"Your mom said something about hard work being rewarded though. If it is possible for us to move classes, how do we do it?"

"We would have to—"

"Mom, I think that's Adam." A voice cut us off as Owen stuck his head out the door. He looked the same as when I last saw him which made sense. It was only a month ago. His long brown hair was pulled back into a ponytail, but now both hands were out of the sling. "There you are. Let's check out Justin's dorm."

"Let's see yours first," Adam replied as he stepped around him. "Do you know who your roommate is?"

"Nah. He's not here. We only came this early because Mom and Dad have work."

I followed Owen inside to see an older couple making up one of the beds. I introduced myself as I took in the C dorm. It wasn't very fancy. They didn't have a bathroom, sitting area, or television. Instead, there were two metal-framed twin-sized beds, two desks, and two trunks. Where they mainly differed from the F dorms is everything in here had been maintained and was spotless. The furniture in my dorm looked like it was fished out of a landfill.

It doesn't matter, Zela. You came here to get close to Derek. Everything else is just details.

We finished our snooping and then headed up to see Justin. He opened his door looking pretty pleased with himself and why not? His room boasted everything ours did but he had his own bathroom and a sitting area minus the television.

"It's not so bad, right?" asked the freckled boy. "Mom went out to pick up some more things, but I like it. Derek and the rest of them were saying they would drop out if they didn't get into the Elite Class, but I don't think it will be that bad to be a B. Plus, once you guys move up, orientation week won't even matter."

"Hope so," Owen said as he hopped up on Justin's desk. "But I still don't understand what happened during orientation. How could you guys miss the practice test?"

I chanced a look at Adam. I didn't know what he told his friends over the summer but at the end of orientation, I felt we made a silent pact not to tell the whole truth. We explained to

Argyle that Cameron, Santiago, and Derek pranked us, but we left the other boys out of it and did not mention a word of the Elite Network. The three of them were already starting the year with two months of detention and I did not want to piss any more people off.

"Cam and Santi pranked us," Adam finally said. "They lured us out into the woods and made us think a student was in trouble, so we ran to find Mom and missed the test."

"Bastards," Owen cursed. "Damn, what's wrong with those guys? They've been messing with us since middle school, but that's too far. Argyle should have kicked them out."

Justin shook his head. "Kick out two Elite students? Something tells me that group can get away with anything."

Unfortunately, no one spoke up to argue with that. All of this was new to me. Bullies, vice principals, and high school hierarchies. I hoped orientation wasn't a glimpse of what the next four years would be like, but I wasn't optimistic.

We hung out in Justin's room a little longer until his mom came back loaded with bags. That was the hint that we should go down and help our own families set up our dorms. When Adam and I returned to our room, it was packed.

"There you are, Zeke," Mom said when I stepped in. "We've gotten you new sheets, pillows, a mattress pad, a trunk, a chair, and a rug."

I blinked. "You did? Where?"

"It's in the car. Go on and bring it up. Miss Moon is going to take me to your vice principal so we can discuss"—she wrinkled her nose as she looked around—"this."

"Mom, you don't have to—"

"I wouldn't mind a chat with her as well," Ryder spoke up smoothly. "We didn't pay attention when we went here, but we were in this school for a few months. I'd like to know what else they're subjecting our son to in this *F* Class."

"I explained the different classes and how it works," Miss Val replied. "It isn't ideal but all students have the same chance to succeed, and as soon as Adam gets the opportunity, he'll be able to move up."

"Let's see if we can't speed that along." Ryder's watch glinted in the artificial light as he buttoned his suit jacket one-handed. Adam didn't have to tell me his dads were rich; I could smell money on them like the cologne Ryder was wearing.

I watched helplessly as Mom, Aunt Bev, Miss Val, and Adam's dads filed out. Mom was on board with me infiltrating Breakbattle in the name of championing female empowerment, but the only thing she cared about more than that was my education. She dropped out her last year of college when she got pregnant with me and she was determined I be an academic success in every way.

If she didn't hate Breakbattle and their gender separation, she might have been another parent demanding I get into the Elite Class. To say she had mixed feelings about sending me to the academy when she saw that F on my placement announcement was an understatement. Argyle not giving in to her wishes might send her over the edge.

Jordan clapped me on the back. "Don't look so nervous, guys. I'm sure your vice principal is used to parents complaining about where their kids get placed."

I gave her a look. "Argyle has never and will never meet a woman like Andronika Manning."

She winced. "That's a good point."

Adam snorted from my other side. "I have to stick up for my dads and their persistence as well. Jaxson once bought out an entire water park because I was scared of losing my family in the crowd. Ezra fired his co-host when he said I shouldn't be allowed to run around on set. Ryder threatened to buy my preschool and have every employee replaced when he found out Derek kept eating my snacks and they hadn't noticed, and Maverick just has to walk into a room and people start doing what he says. They're tough."

"Goodness," Jordan said. "Do your parents just swoop in and make everything better for you? I wish that was my life."

Adam laughed, taking that as good-naturedly as he took everything. "My siblings and I are very lucky. Most only get two awesome parents. We got five."

I tuned them out as I focused on one part of Adam's speech. A vision of a tiny Derek stealing Adam's crackers and escaping onto the jungle gym played in my mind.

I wonder when he'll get here, I thought. *I wonder if he meant the things he said on the last day of orientation.*

Swallowed up in my thoughts, I strode out of the room to rescue my things from Mom's car. I made it halfway down the hall before I heard Adam and Jordan behind me, deep in conversation.

They caught up to me by the time I reached the front lawn and together we brought up the stuff from their shopping spree. Forty-five minutes later and my side of the room went from prison-chic to only mildly uninhabitable. Mom bought me a memory foam mattress pad, comfy royal blue sheets, a matching rug and foldable chair that we barely squeezed into the corner of the room and a new lockable trunk. The old one I moved in front of my chair as a makeshift desk.

Jordan stepped back and surveyed our work. "Not bad. Aunt Dronika is a lot, but you have to give her credit, she doesn't let anyone screw you around."

I cracked a smile. "She definitely does not. I think Adam and I could swap some serious stories."

He chuckled as he flopped down on his bed. As promised, his side was already done. His bed was covered in nice forest green sheets and his duffel bags unpacked and lying by the trunk, but compared to my side, it was pretty bare.

"I'm surprised your mom and dads haven't hooked you up too, Adam," Jordan said, voicing my thoughts.

"My dads wanted to but Mom said no. There's a whole thing about students bringing in stuff from home and she didn't want me to worry about it."

"What?" I froze in the middle of taking a seat on my bed. "What do you mean? Am I going to get in trouble?"

He shook his head, making his curls flop into his eyes. "No, you won't. They can't stop your parents buying things for you, but not all the kids have wealthy folks who can—"

"—transform these dumps," Jordan finished.

"Exactly. She said it's better not to have to deal with jealousy in my own class on top of everything else."

"That's a good point," I mumbled, chewing my lip. If Breakbattle wanted us to feel the harsh separation of the classes, then those who suffered wouldn't look kindly on those who don't, especially if they were supposed to be in it together.

I sighed. It didn't matter. There was no way I would convince Mom to take it back and I didn't want her to anyway. I was already feeling better sinking into my warm sheets. I just wouldn't go around bragging, which wasn't something I would do anyway.

Jordan clapped. "Since we're done, you guys want to show me around until they kick the families out? We went on the tour in the summer but they only showed us the Elite classes and stuff. I want to see life on the F side."

"Me too," said Adam. "But the class wings will be locked until tomorrow. We can walk around the grounds though."

That was an easy trade-off and we headed out. We wandered around, going in and out of the gyms and fields, as the rest of Breakbattle's students arrived—old and new. Justin and Owen joined our group when their parents left and we found ourselves goofing off on the bleachers in front of the track.

"So after I said bye to Mom," Justin said, "I came in through the administration doors and spotted Principal Whittaker and Vice Principal Argyle talking to your parents, Adam, and a bald woman going on about the mind being a source of power."

Two pairs of eyes swung to me as I pinched the bridge of my nose. "That would be the woman who gave me life."

"She's your mom?" Justin leaned back, looking me up and down. "That explains a lot."

"Hey!" I cried, laughing. I shoved his shoulder and almost sent him toppling off the bench. "She's not thrilled about me being in F Class and who can blame her? As she said many times over the last month, she did not devote years of her life to fill my intellectual well for me to not be recognized for my talents."

Owen chuckled. "Mom said the same thing but more like, 'I didn't spend all that money on tutors and private lessons for those bastards to label my kid a C.' She really wasn't happy they wouldn't make an exception for my arm."

Beep. Beep.

We all instinctively looked down but it was Jordan who pulled her phone out of her pocket. "It's my mom," she said aloud. "It's almost time for them to leave and she wants us to say goodbye."

I got to my feet at the same time as Adam. "The next text will be from my folks," he said. "Let's go."

We tromped across the field and slipped into the main building for the cafeteria. The room was a riot of noise, good-byes, and well wishes for a new semester. Students were allowed to go home on the weekends if they had the option, but still people were squeezing the stuffing out of their kids like we were going to war.

Aunt Bev subjected me to the same treatment the second she got her hands on me. I grunted as she crushed me to her chest, burying my nose in her unique scent of jasmine and saw-dust. "Be good, Zee. I love you."

"Hmm hm hmm," I replied.

"Just keep your head down and focus on your studies."

"Your studies are your first priority"—hands seized me and tugged me free—"and I've spoken to your principal and he has assured me this F Class nonsense need only be temporary. You do whatever is necessary to fix that situation."

"Yes, Mom," Jordan and I said at the same time.

I whipped my head around and gave her a withering look. She smiled back innocently.

Mom lowered her voice. "In the meantime, keep your eyes and ears open. Try to befriend more of the girls and especially stick close to this Melody you were telling me about. She sounds very impressive."

"I will." I got Mom to let me enroll under the idea of helping with the book, I had to play along.

"Goodbye, my only one. Call me if you want to come home this weekend."

I hid a smile as Mom kissed my forehead. Her goodbye didn't look as smothering or weepy as the others, but this was the equivalent for my mother. We had spent the last fifteen years practically glued at the hip traveling and homeschooling. She never had to "miss" me or share me with anyone else. I think it was hitting her how weird it was to say goodbye to me.

Mom stepped back and Jordan pounced. "Of course, Zee's coming home. He promised." She hugged me tight. "Remember everything I said and be careful."

I hugged her back. "Don't worry about me. You just kill it at school this week and tell me all about it when I get home."

We exchanged more goodbyes, Aunt Bev strangled me a couple more times, and I fought not to choke up. Crying would do nothing for my reputation.

"Attention, everyone."

The call drew our attention to the front of the room. Argyle stood before the doors with Principal Whittaker at her side.

"I'm afraid it's time for parents to say their final goodbyes," said the vice principal, "and for the freshmen to gather in the auditorium."

Whittaker leveled us with a grin. "Your lives at Breakbattle are about to begin."

Chapter Two

Adam and I walked behind a group of boys as we streamed into the auditorium. This was it. The academy and its battle system were finally going to be explained to the wide-eyed young freshmen before they were thrown to the wolves.

I peered around as I followed Adam to a seat near the front. There were so many faces moving up, down, and all over the place that it was hard to pick out the one I was looking for.

"Look, it's Owen. Let's sit over there."

I veered off without stopping my search. *Where is he? Where's Derek?*

Adam and I sat down on the third row from the stage next to Owen and Justin. On the platform, the staff were filling up the seats and prepping to start the presentation.

"Did you guys get to meet some upperclassmen?"

Justin's question made me turn my attention to him. "None other than the charmers we met during orientation."

"I was talking to one of the juniors on my floor and he said—"

"Sup, dickheads." The greeting told me before I turned around who had plopped down next to me.

Derek.

Here he was after all of this time, and it was clear summer had only been good to him. There was a pleasant tan clinging to his skin and a grin on his lips that I rarely saw the last time we were together.

"Did you miss me?" he asked.

The boys were quick with their response.

"Nope."

"Not even a little."

"Fuck off."

"Yes." The word popped out of my mouth so fast there was no chance to hold it back. I flushed hot as Derek lifted a brow. "I-I meant I missed everyone," I rushed to say. "I missed the academy and my friends and... everyone."

He laughed. "You serious? What's to miss? I wouldn't even be here if my dad wasn't making me."

"You mean you didn't want to come back?"

"And deal with the load of bullshit that's about to come barreling at us full speed? Not interested." He cocked his head, peering at me. "I'm surprised you came back. I'll take my detention for what I pulled on you and Moon, but you better not think Cameron is going to let this go. He will make you pay for ratting him out."

"I don't care about him. He can do his worst. I can take it."

Derek shook his head. "You've got balls, Zeke. You're naïve, but you've got balls."

He said that with a slight smile, so I was ignoring the naïve part and taking it as a compliment. The truth was Cameron had no chance of scaring me away as long as Derek was here. I would face whatever he threw at me.

"But you are here," I said, "so I'm guessing that means you got into the Elite Class."

He inclined his head. "Yep. If you're wondering, so did Cole, Michael, Landon, and Zach."

My hand flew to my cheek at the mention of that last name. "How do you know?"

"Move-in day for Elite students was yesterday. Last night there was a formal dinner for us, the faculty, and some of the alumni."

"Formal dinner for Elites only? But that's not—"

"Fair?" he cut in. "Get used to saying that."

I sat back, letting it go. Derek could go to all the dinners he wanted with the treacherous—and violent—Elite boys. I had bigger things to worry about.

We didn't say much more as we waited for things to get started. I perked up when Argyle finally stepped up to the podium.

"Hello, gentlemen, and welcome to your first year at Break-battle Academy." Whoops and cheers broke out and the staff joined in with polite applause. "I know you're as excited as I am to see you grow and achieve your potential, and now you will find out exactly how you will do so." She gazed over our heads. "Pass out the handbooks, please."

I glanced over my shoulder and spotted two guys with cardboard boxes coming down the row.

"Everything I tell you here today will be outlined in your handbooks, so there is no excuse not to know the rules or how our school functions," she said. "After this assembly, you will return to your rooms to find your uniforms have been delivered. I want to be clear that every minute from this point forward, you must be in uniform. The only exceptions are gym class and physical battles. Even if you've elected to stay on campus over the weekend, you will wear your uniform. But on the weekends, you can wear the casual version to allow you more freedom to play and relax. If you are out of uniform, you will receive an automatic detention. No excuses."

I shifted in my seat, looking around. I'd never lived the uniform life, but that sounded pretty strict even to a homeschooler. From the looks on the other boys' faces, I wasn't the only one who thought so.

"Your uniforms will denote your class and your class will be like your family. You will share the same teacher, the same dormitory, and the same lessons. All privileges that apply to one will apply to all in your class equally. You will have the same chances and tools to succeed, but it will be up to you to do something about it. Do you have any questions?"

No one moved. There wasn't so much as a cough.

"Come now," she pressed. "The purpose of this assembly is to ensure all of your questions are answered so that everyone starts this year on the right foot." She swept over the room and landed on someone. "Yes, Mr. Johansson?"

"My parents live in Sweden," said an accented voice. "What do I do on the weekends?"

"Excellent question. We are different from other boarding schools in that we allow students to leave on non-school days, but this must be done by a parent or guardian. The only exception is for students who are eighteen. If they do not physically come to the office to sign you out, you must stay here. Of course, you will be fed and a full staff will be on hand to look out for you. To make this enjoyable for you, we frequently hold movie nights, themed dinners, dances, and other events for our weekenders."

Wow, I thought. *That does sound nice.*

"These are open to those who earn the privilege."

I sighed, deflating. Of course, it was.

"Any more questions before I move on?" Argyle prompted. After a pause, she pointed to someone behind me. "Yes, Mr. Tims?"

"How does the battle system work?"

I caught her lips quirk up in a smile. "You're ahead of me, Mr. Tims. We're going to discuss that next." She waved at us. "If you open your books to page twenty-seven, you can follow along as I explain."

The sound of flipped pages filled the room as a white screen was lowered behind the staff. No one uttered a peep. This was what we really wanted to know.

"Alright. The fundamentals of a battle are this: the challenger will choose the mental test and the challengee will choose the physical test. This is done for a very simple reason and it is your safety. We cannot have a person who can't swim challenged to a swimming battle and have to choose between damaging their grade or drowning. Your safety is our first priority and I speak for all of us when I say, do not push yourself past the breaking point. If you need help, you can come to a member of staff at any time."

I wondered if the name Becca Taylor was going through anyone else's mind. I believed Argyle when she said she cared about our well-being for the simple fact it was hard to tout Breakbattle as the best school in the world if it drove kids to suicide.

"As I was saying," she continued. "The challengee chooses the physical test, but what if they choose a swimming battle and the challenger can't swim? Well, the person who issues the challenge is free to rescind it without penalty at any time before the battle becomes official."

I nodded along, absorbing every word like there would be a test.

Argyle clicked the next slide. "How is a battle made official? Once the challenge is issued and accepted, both parties will report to their teachers and tell them the terms. If it's within the rules, the next stop is to the appropriate coach and times will be set for each battle. Both your teacher or teachers must be present for the battle. After the physical test, they will calculate the results and tell you the winner."

My eyes flicked from the screen to the handbook, following along. As promised, everything she was saying was written for me to read. Despite myself, a sliver of appreciation was working its way through me at how elegantly they had prepared this system. Don't get me wrong, it was nuts, but still... impressive.

"Battles are held between two p.m. and six p.m.," Argyle said as she moved on to the next slide. "Monday through Friday after school. Battles must be held the week they are approved, but if a battle is issued on a Friday, they will be held on the Monday following. This is to give all students roughly the same amount of time to prepare for a battle. Any questions about what I've said?"

No one spoke.

"Okay, then I'll move on to the rules. Battles are not free-for-alls. They are instrumental in helping you achieve new heights and should be treated as such. Do not issue battles you're not prepared for simply because you can. You waste yours, your classmates', and your educators' time.

"In that vein, battles are not to be used as a means to enact or prompt harm to a student physically, emotionally, or academically. They are also never to be held over money. Is that clear?"

"Yes, Mrs. Argyle," we chorused.

She pointed up at a sentence that had been bolded, underlined, and italicized on the screen. "Battles are challenged for one thing and one thing only. You do not challenge someone for a spot on every field trip, you challenge for a spot on one field trip. You do not issue a battle for his library time for a whole week, you do so for one day. One," she repeated. "Everyone here has worked hard to get what they have and I have no desire to see it all stripped away on the basis of one battle any more than you do."

I bobbed my head in silent agreement. I had to admit, I didn't walk on to this campus with much faith in the staff who enforced this system. Hearing what happened to Becca Taylor and the fact that they had chosen to separate the boys and girls instead of doing away with battles, made me doubt how much they cared about us. But it did seem like rules were in place to lessen the chance of abuse.

Argyle asked if anyone had questions again and someone stood up. "Is there a list of privileges or something so we know what we can or can't battle over?"

"That would be on page thirty-nine." We hurriedly found the page while she clicked to the right slide. "We have listed in detail what every class has earned so you can take advantage of them beginning now. If we introduce something new, which does happen as we have a wonderful network of alumni who offer gifts and treats to the students, we'll tell you right away who will be bestowed the privilege."

I stiffened at the word network even though she wasn't speaking of the one I was thinking about.

"Last year, Sean Beckinsale, former alumna and owner of Beckinsale Yachts, invited five seniors to join him on a two-night trip off the coast where he shared his tips for managing a multibillion-dollar business. These spots were awarded to the senior members of the business club first, so it was their privilege to keep or lose in a battle."

I flipped through as she spoke, skimming through the list of privileges for each class. It was no surprise that the list of things for the Elite Class was a mile long. Seriously, it took up five pages before I got to the A Class. I kept going through B, C, D, and then finally—

My mouth fell open as I took in the word beneath "F Class Privileges."

"None?" I whispered. "How can there be none?"

"What did you expect?"

I looked up at Derek.

"There are no privileges for being at the bottom," he added.

I pressed my lips together rather than say anything. It wasn't the lack of privileges so much as the realization that if I wanted to get anything in this school, I would have to battle for it. There truly was no opting out.

"Now, I want to address the final, and most important, element of the battle system before I continue to dorm rules." Argyle lifted her head as she looked out over the crowd. "You've heard it said that everything in Breakbattle is yours for the taking and that doesn't end at privileges.

"The class you have been placed in is not the class where you must stay. If you show marked improvement and your teachers and coaches are on board, you are free to participate in the tournament."

Tournament?

I quickly flipped through the book, searching for that word.

"Tournaments are not to be taken lightly. An individual can challenge a student to one, and only one tournament, during their time here, so they must be certain of their skills and ability to win. They must get the approval of their teachers, coaches, as well as me and Principal Whittaker.

"If we accept, the tournament will take place at the end of the year before finals week. You and the challenger must compete in every subject and sport trial just as you did during orientation week, and if the challenger wins, they will trade places with the one they challenge and begin the school year in their new class. This means seniors cannot participate in tournaments, but everyone else is encouraged to try.

"Breakbattle is not about maintaining the status quo. Our goal is simply to see every student reach their full potential. If you are in the B, C, or"—Argyle's eyes met mine—"F Class and you think you don't belong. Prove it."

I held her gaze steadily. I got the message loud and clear. She wouldn't be swayed by my mother or anyone else. If I wanted out of the F Class, this was the only way.

Argyle opened it up to questions and was hit with almost a dozen. I tuned it out as I considered my options.

Mom expected me to get out of the F Class. That I knew, but if I was understanding it correctly, challenging another student to a tournament meant ripping them out of the class they worked hard to be in and tossing them into F in my place. Could I do that to someone?

"Okay, everyone. Dorm rules," Argyle announced, jarring me back to reality. "It goes without saying that girls are never to be in the boys' dormitory. There is no reason they should be on this side of campus at all."

I listened with half an ear. I wasn't about to sneak any girls into my dorm.

The vice principal went through all the rules and policies and then wrapped things up with a Q & A session addressed to the whole faculty. At one point, Miss Val stepped up to the podium after one guy asked why we had mandatory therapy sessions.

An hour later, we were dismissed for lunch and I wandered out of the room, nose stuck in the handbook. I peeped someone fall in next to me as I read.

"What did you think?" asked Adam.

I answered without looking up. "I like that they took the time to answer our questions, but it's still a lot to process. We don't get any privileges, Adam."

"It sucks for sure."

"And can you believe the privileges the Elite Class gets?" I continued. "It says here they can have food *delivered* during meal times."

"Derek, you'll love that."

I yanked my head up. I hadn't noticed him walking on Adam's other side.

"You said the food here tasted like sunbaked shit covered in rancid milk. A vivid description worthy of your status."

"And I was dead on," he said, grinning. "I am going to love ordering out."

Shaking my head, I kept reading the list. "On your birthdays the Elite can request a *party*? Seriously?"

"The day I entered the world should be celebrated," Derek commented. "It's a fact I've made it better just by being in it."

It was a feat stopping myself from rolling my eyes. If being considered Derek's friend meant listening to his nonstop self-love parade, then this was going to be a long four years.

"Elites get first dibs on field trips. Elites are offered the captaincy of sports teams first and if no candidates are suitable, then it is to be offered to A Class students and so forth. Elites are entitled to all library time slots from six a.m. to midnight."

I quickly checked the other classes. "While A Class gets six to ten. B Class gets one to eight. C Class gets two to six. D Class gets two to four and F Class gets no time slots at all!" I snapped the book shut. "What are we supposed to do if we need a book?"

"Mom says teachers are required to give us any books or materials we need for a test or project," Adam said. "But any supplemental reading or if we just want to go in there to study, we have to battle for it."

I tossed my head as we crossed through the doors of the lunchroom. That was going to be the answer to every question from here on out. I had better get used to it.

Together, the three of us stepped up to the lunch line. There was something different about today compared to orientation. Now, the room was filled with boys from every grade. The upperclassmen were here, including—

My shoulders tensed when I spotted Cameron in his favorite spot near the head table. He was surrounded by his usual circle of Elites. The five guys who kidnapped us out of bed and tormented us for their little club. Keeping with the rules, they were wearing their uniform with their Es emblazoned proudly on their chests.

I looked away before they caught me watching them.

Slowly, we made our way up the line and collected bowtie pasta, green salad, a fruit cup, a carton of milk, and a small brownie square for dessert.

Derek grimaced at his tray. "Disgusting what they make us eat. No wonder Foster only eats the apples. I should get something delivered now."

Derek went on as we found a table near the windows, sat down, and tucked in. Twenty minutes in, I was stuck between happy he was serious about eating lunch together and wanting to tell him we would never eat lunch together again.

Derek took a bite of his salad and gagged. "What the hell is on this thing?!"

"It's Italian dressing," Adam said.

"It's sour vomit. My chef only makes me homemade vinaigrettes."

A groan ripped from my throat. "Hush and eat this!" I picked up my brownie and plopped it on his plate. "You must like it because it's the only thing you ate without complaining."

"Thanks, Zeke." Derek tore a bite off my brownie with no hesitation. "But I don't complain. I explain why things are not the way they should be. There's a difference."

I tried to stop it, but a laugh escaped my lips. "You're one of a kind, aren't you, Derek Grayson?"

He winked.

Somehow, the mood shifted and we fell into a nice conversation.

"My family and I went up the coast this summer," I told them. "I've been to about a dozen major cities, but New York City wasn't one of them. We decided to make it a whole trip and saw a show on Broadway, visited the museums, walked around the city. It was the first trip Jordan and I took together and we had so much fun."

Derek opened his mouth.

"And don't you dare say anything about her being hot, ask me for her number, or call me a cousin-lover."

He closed his mouth again, smirking away.

"What did you do, Adam?"

"We went on a cruise to the Cayman Islands. It's the last trip we'll take for a while since Mom is due to have the baby soon."

Derek hummed. "My mom was on location in the Caribbean too. She brought me along and I hooked up with a few of the extras."

My eyes drifted over his shoulder as he went into detail. I had been doing that every five minutes, but this time I found them almost right away.

Cole and Michael were sitting at a table near the doors. The table sat ten chairs, but all were empty except for the two they occupied. I watched as people veered around them, searching out other free seats without bothering to ask if they could sit. The two were in their own world, amused about something that was making Michael laugh and Cole crack a smile. For a moment during orientation, I was in that world. I wondered if that was still true.

My eyes sought Landon next. He wasn't alone. His table was full with boys but they dimmed in comparison to him. I had looked up his father's fashion line over the summer and I knew the dusky gold knitted cardigan he wore was one of his dad's creations. I wished I could see what color his eyes were, but his head was bent over his phone.

Did the three of them hate me for giving up Cam and Santi?

None of them were friends with those two, but the fact remained that Derek was the only person to come speak to me after everything went down. The others hadn't said a word so I didn't know how we left things.

That's not necessarily true, I thought as I sought out one more face. *I know how I left things with you.*

My eyes narrowed to slits as I gazed at Zachary Fields. In my whole life, I had never been hit and then this guy punches me to protect who we had every reason to believe was a killer. My insides burned thinking that Cameron, Santiago, and Derek had been punished while Zach skipped home free and clear.

"You pissed he made it?"

I blinked. "What? Who?"

"Fields," said Derek. He was looking in the same direction. "He got into the Elite Class and the Network. It's messed up."

"Yes, it is," I whispered.

"He got what he threw his best friend under the bus for," Derek went on. "Look at him lapping up the attention like a dehydrated whore."

Adam was right about his similes. He did go for descriptive.

"He's got all-new Elite buddies now."

I glanced at Adam, seeing him lower his head. Zachary meant nothing to me, but the two of them had been friends for a long time. I could only imagine how much his betrayal hurt him, Justin, and Owen.

"Are they all Elite?" I asked.

"Yep. There's me, Cole, Michael, Landon, and Zach. The rest are at Zach's table. Lars Johansson, Wyatt Wharton, Jose Dimas, Sullivan Porter, and Rhys Lewis. The ten boys in the school who'll have everything worth taking."

"Not that anyone will."

Every molecule in my body froze. There was no mistaking the voice that slithered into my ear.

The hairs on my neck stood on end as a shadow fell over me. So wrapped up was I in the new freshmen Elite, I took my eyes off the ones I truly needed to be worried about.

"What are you doing with them, Grayson? You're Elite now. This isn't your table."

Derek bared his teeth. "I'll tell you for the last fucking time. You don't tell me what to do. I'll sit wherever I want."

"Is that it? You're acting tough, or... you're feeling guilty? You feel bad these two turned snitch for your sorry ass and now the big, bad Derek Grayson has grown a conscience."

I didn't need to turn around to sense Cameron was enjoying this and it made the bile rise in my throat. I grabbed my milk and took a sip to wash out the taste. What made someone this beautiful so hideous inside?

Derek's expression smoothed out. "I'm not being tough or guilty. I just don't want anything to do with you. No one does. That's why the only friends you have are afraid of you or in deep with your father."

"That's rich coming from you. The only friend you've ever had sold you out to the media for a couple of bucks."

Derek fell quiet. I couldn't name the look in his eyes as he stared at Cameron, but it rattled me straight to my core. "That's enough, Cam," I spoke up. "Leave us alone."

"Look at that. Your pint-sized protector speaks."

"Be very careful, Dupre," Derek said softly. "You forget I know things about your father and his business."

"My dad's never done anything wrong!"

"I'll let you go on believing that if you turn around and walk your ass out of this cafeteria."

I heard a scoff. "You think you're protected because your daddy is high up in the Network, and you might be right, but that doesn't apply"—something flashed in front of me and my milk went flying—"to these two."

I bolted up, shouting as ice-cold milk went in my eyes, nose, and hair.

"Don't think this is the end," a silken voice said. "I've got more planned for you snitches."

I stood there, gasping, as every eye in the room fell on me. There was a momentary lull and then titters broke out. Within five seconds, half the room was laughing their heads off.

Classes hadn't even begun and the target had been drawn on my back.

"SORRY ABOUT TODAY."

I closed the handbook and rested it on the comforter. Adam and I were safely in our rooms, sitting up in bed.

"It wasn't your fault," I replied. "Honestly, I expected backlash and I'll take a face full of milk over getting punched or coerced into being an accomplice to murder any day."

He shook his head. "You must be missing homeschooling right about now. You probably think we're all insane."

"No, I don't." I wasn't feeling too warm and fuzzy toward Cameron or his minions, but I couldn't say the same for Derek and Adam who walked me out of the cafeteria or Owen and Justin who came to check on me after I got cleaned up and joined our table when we went back down for dinner.

"I want to be at Breakbattle," I said. "I made my choices and I'll handle whatever Cameron throws at me because I'm not going anywhere."

He sighed as he burrowed down into his sheets. "Then I guess we'd better get some sleep. First day of F Class, here we come."

MY PHONE BUZZED BENEATH the covers, gently waking me without alerting Adam. Silently, I slipped out of bed, picked up the bundle on my chair, and tiptoed out of the dorm.

There wasn't a soul in the hallway, but there wouldn't be at five in the morning. I wasn't taking any chances of being discovered.

I walked the length of the hall to the single door on the end. I knew what it was like in here from my trip the night before. The space was dingy, the tiles cracked, and there was a musty, sweaty smell that forced me to use the bathroom and brush my teeth quickly.

The urinals and stalls were situated in front of the mirrors, but the showers were in the back. Six showers on either side that were thankfully hidden behind curtains. I had been having nightmares about the open shower locker room madness where everything hung out. I didn't have a clue what I would have done if I walked in on that.

I passed through one of the curtains and went through the long process of undressing, unwrapping my bindings, and then finally freeing myself of the wig. Then I took the longest, hottest shower I could stand. The water was great for my tense muscles and I soon relaxed and let my stress about the new year wash down the drain.

Adam was stirring when I returned to the dorm fresh and dressed.

"What's going on?" he grumbled. He squinted at me as he pushed himself up. "You're dressed? Why didn't you wake me?"

"Because your alarm doesn't go off for another ten minutes. I just wanted to get a start on the day."

He yawned so wide I feared his jaw would crack. "I'll get up now. We can go down to the F hall and finally see what the next year of our life will be like."

Adam didn't take long to get ready. I waited for him outside as he got dressed, watching the other F students emerge from their rooms and shuffle to the bathroom or the exit. I tried to covertly check them out as they passed by me. I recognized a few faces from orientation. The unfamiliar faces I pegged as upperclassmen but it was hard to be sure.

Breakbattle didn't separate the dorms by grade. They did it by class. Freshmen, sophomores, juniors, and seniors were all on this floor and with identical khaki pants, black blazers, and the purple F on our chest, we melded together.

"Ready?"

I shook myself as Adam closed our door behind him. "I'm ready."

Together, we followed a group out of the door to the main building. They went one way at the fork in the hallway while we went the other. Our schedules had been sitting on top of our uniforms when we returned to our rooms the day before and our orders were to go straight to class instead of the cafeteria.

Adam and I traveled down a long hallway. As we went, the photos of famed alumni got fewer and fewer until the walls were bare. We rounded a corner and found ourselves in front of double doors with one letter hanging over the frame.

F.

Through the glass, we spotted the other freshmen milling around, talking, and going in and out of the classrooms.

The first day of school had started.

I consulted our schedule as we pushed through the doors. "We're in classroom one with Mr. Dawson."

"I think it's at the end."

Together we slipped through the crowd, searching out our new class. I didn't know what was going through Adam's head, or mine for that matter. It was a riot of conflicting emotions as I looked around.

I didn't know what regular high schools looked like to compare, but I could compare the rest of the academy and it was nothing like this. The floors of the gyms gleamed while these were scuffed and marked. Chandeliers hung in the cafeteria while the lights above us flickered with bulbs on their last breath.

"This is it." Adam stepped up to the last door on the end and pushed through. I followed him in at a slower pace, taking in the scene.

"Alright, alright. Grab some breakfast and take a seat anywhere," said the man in a tweed coat. He was standing in the back of the room next to a table covered with food. "We have a lot to get through before we jump in."

The classroom was bigger than I thought it would be, but that made sense since it needed to fit the thirty-five— no, the thirty-seven desks I counted. At the front of the room was a chalkboard, the teacher's desk, and about a dozen cardboard boxes.

Adam set his bag down on a desk toward the front and then headed to the food table as ordered. I chose the seat behind him and went to do the same. There were already a few boys going down the table. Mr. Dawson handed out plates with one hand and consulted his clipboard with the other.

"You are?"

"Adam Moon."

"Ah, yes. Welcome, Mr. Moon. And you?" he asked without looking up.

"I'm Zeke Manning."

"Got you right here, Mr. Manning. Grab some breakfast and sit down."

Dutifully, I scooped the scrambled eggs and hash browns onto my paper plate and grabbed a bottle of apple juice. We retook our seats and started digging in as the class filled up. The noise level grew as more people came in and friends caught up.

"Hey, Marco, sit here."

"What did you do this summer?"

"I think I left my phone at your place."

Two guys stepped in front of us. "Can you believe they put us in F? The placement test was ninth grade stuff and up. How is it fair testing us on stuff we haven't been taught yet?" The chairs scraped against the tile as they pulled them out. "Isn't it messed up? Hey? I'm talking to you."

"What?" My head snapped up. My new desk neighbor stared back at me. Even folded up in his desk I could see he was tall. His brown hair was on the long side and gelled into submission, but none of that was what was tickling my memory.

How do I know you...?

Then it came to me. "Wait. You're the guy who almost started a fight when the other boy crossed into your lane during the swimming trial."

"Yep," he said easily. "And you're the cross-dresser who wore the girls' wrestling suit."

"That's me."

He laughed. "The name's Tanner Grady and this is Nico Kazan."

The guy in front of him waved. I recognized him from orientation week, but we never spoke. He was cute with his hair shaved close to the scalp and a dimple in one cheek.

"Where you two from?" Tanner asked.

"I'm from Chesterfield," I replied.

He frowned. "What? Then how don't we know you? Where did you go to middle school?"

"I was homeschooled."

"Oh, cool. That makes sense. What about you?" He swung his attention to Adam. "Homeschooled?"

"I'm from Evergreen. Went to school there."

His jaw slackened. "You what? How the hell did you end up here? I thought all you Evergreen kids bought your way into the higher classes. Are you the one unlucky bastard from that place that isn't rich?"

Scowling, I opened my mouth to defend him.

"No, I'm one of the lucky bastards," Adam replied, not skipping a beat. "But I was hoping to ride into the A Class on nepotism since my mom works here. But damn, I should have gone with your idea. Bribing was definitely the smarter play."

The two burst out laughing. "You should have, man," Tanner joked. "Maybe you do belong here with us dummies."

I shook my head, hiding a smile. Why was this guy so good with people?

"You got a point about the placement test being ninth and up," Adam went on. "It's not fair if you've never been taught that stuff."

Nico smacked the desk. "That's what we're saying. They set us up to fail and then punish us for it."

I inclined my head. I never thought of it like that, but less than an hour in the F Wing and I was certainly seeing why the boys would think they were being punished.

"Okay, gentlemen, listen up."

Our conversation drew to a halt as Mr. Dawson walked up to the front. He planted himself before his desk and swept his eyes over us.

"You can keep eating your breakfast while I speak. We have a lot to go through today." He clapped. "First, my name is Sandy Dawson and I'll be your teacher for the next year. Yes, Sandy is my real name and yes my parents wanted a girl."

Chuckles broke out and I felt myself relaxing. For my first ever teacher, this short man in the tweed didn't seem so bad.

"Unlike other high schools, I will be your teacher for every subject, so get used to those chairs. You'll be in them every day, all day, except for when we move to the lab or you have PE. As you can imagine, that's a lot of papers, tests, and assignments to grade. This means the time to find me and organize a battle will be on Mondays when I'm procrastinating and pushing my grading to later in the week."

That got another laugh, but still I filed that tidbit away.

"These are your textbooks." He gestured at the boxes next to him. "I have to sign them out to you as they have to be handed in at the end for the next year. If you do not return your book, you will be charged for a replacement.

"According to your schedule, you have English I, Algebra I, Biology, and U.S. History for your academic classes this semester. Next semester, we switch to Spanish I, Computer Science, Public Speaking, and Art. Physical classes are every day, five days a week. Basketball on Monday. Swimming on Tuesday. Soccer on Wednesday. Track on Thursday. Wrestling on Friday. Any questions?"

No one raised their hand, except me.

"Yes, Mr....?"

"Zeke Manning."

"Yes, Zeke?"

"What if you're higher than Algebra I?"

"Higher than Algebra I?" he repeated. "What do you mean?"

"Mom and I were studying integral and differential calculus before we moved here. Will we study that?"

His brows shot up to his receding hairline. "As a freshman? Of course not. F Class students study *precalculus* in their senior year."

"But then how do I take calculus? Is there another class? Do I have to battle to get in?"

"I'm afraid it doesn't work that way for academic subjects. If you want to be in another math class, you have to win a tournament and move up."

I made a face. "But that can't be right. Shouldn't I take the courses that are right for me?"

Mr. Dawson looked at me steadily. "You were placed in the F Class, Zeke. These are the right courses for you."

I rocked back like he slapped me. What was that supposed to mean? Did he not believe I could do calculus?

Dawson turned his attention to the class. "Any more questions?"

No one spoke.

"Good. Then finish eating, throw out your trash, and we'll get started."

My hand drifted up to my chest as the boys got up to follow his directions. This F was more than a patch or a class.

It was a brand.

DING! DING! DING!

"That's the lunch bell," Dawson said over the chorus of pushed-back chairs and slammed textbooks. "After lunch, you have biology, history, and then you'll report to the basketball gym."

I left my things behind and followed Adam out of the room. The hallway was packed as students streamed out heading for the cafeteria.

"Sorry about the calc thing," Adam piped up. "I guess you're stuck for Spanish too since you're fluent."

I sighed. "I didn't think of that. Dawson won't really have me sitting there reciting my colors when I can read whole chapter books in Spanish... right?"

He shrugged. "He's just one guy. I doubt he's got time to teach different levels to each student."

"See. We said this place was screwed up."

I jumped. Swinging around, I discovered Nico and Tanner trailing us like it was no big deal.

"Can you really do calc?" Tanner asked.

"My mom and I were studying it. I actually really like it. Especially integral calculus and determining the graph of a function. You divide the graph into pieces and—"

Tanner held up a hand. "Don't have a clue what you're talking about, Zeke, but I'm convinced. Math period is going to be real boring for you."

"I could talk to Argyle and Whittaker," I said. "They know my situation. There must be something they could do."

Nico scoffed. "You think they'll listen to an F kid?"

Disappointment settled like lead in my stomach. I wasn't the only one feeling the weight of this letter.

The boys started talking about something else while I chewed over my predicament. Even if a tournament was the only way to get into a calc class, that wasn't something I could do until the end of the year. What did I do until then?

Together we headed to the lunchroom, joining with other classes as we went. Today's lunch was a cheeseburger, selection of fruit, and baked chips. I collected my lunch from the server with a thank you.

Tanner stepped up behind me. "Tanner Grady."

"Of course, dear," said the lunch lady. "This one is for you." She bent down and pulled out a tray.

"Thanks, Miss Darlene." He turned away and caught me looking. "Can't eat wheat. I break out in hives—start vomiting. It's not pretty."

"Wow. Good to know."

I stepped off the line and went to find a table. Or I should say *we* walked off to find a table. For some reason, Tanner and Nico were right on our heels.

I looked at them in confusion when they set their trays down. Were we... friends now? Was that how boys did it? They just glommed on to each other and went with it? In my experience, girls made you work a lot harder. Jordan didn't even like me at first. She kept pushing me over in the playpen and sticking her tongue out at me when I cried. She didn't warm up to me until we were five.

Well, you're a boy now, Zela. Just follow their lead.

We sat down and started digging in.

"Dickheads!"

I stifled a sigh. There was only one person that could be.

"Feast your eyes and only your eyes."

Something smacked down on the table as the chair next to me was pulled out.

"What?!" Nico cried. "How did you get that?"

That was a super-sized cheese pizza with honking slices of pepperoni and dripping with just enough grease to let you know it was sinfully good.

"Elite Class, baby. That's how we roll." Derek leaned over and picked up a slice. Cradling it with both hands, he guided the mouthwatering pizza up to my face. "Jealous, Zeke? You want some of this, don't you? Smell that baked dough and fragrant mozzarella. Stuck with that limp, gray meat while I eat all the pizza." He waved it up and down—so close I could lean forward and take a bite. "You know you want it. Don't you? Hm, hm, hm."

I gave Derek a deadpan look. "I don't want to be your friend anymore."

He tossed his head back, guffawing. "Too late for that."

"You know, I do want some." Adam tore off a slice and shoved it in his mouth before Derek could blink.

"Hey!"

He grinned at him through a mouthful of cheese. "You stole my animal crackers every day for a month. You owe me."

To my surprise, Derek chuckled. "When you put it like that, I owe you more than one." He pushed the box across the table. "You guys can have some too."

"Seriously?" asked Nico. "Thanks, man."

I snatched one up before he could change his mind.

"I can't have any," said Tanner. "Wheat allergy."

"Raw deal. I'll get a gluten-free pizza next time."

"Yeah? That's cool of you. So you Elite guys aren't all ass-holes."

Derek shook his head. "Oh no, they are. Every single one of them. I'm the only nice one."

I almost choked on my pizza. "Derek Grayson, if lies really could make your pants catch fire, you'd be a pile of smoldering ash right now."

"Oh ho," he cried. "That's how it is? After all I've done for you?"

"*To* me," I corrected

"Well, if I'm not nice, give back the pizza." He made a swipe for it and I lurched back.

"Touch this and I'm not responsible for what happens next," I threatened, but it was impossible to keep a straight face. In about three seconds, I lost it and Derek wasn't much better. He laughed and for a brief moment I saw that smile so like the one from the very first time I laid eyes on him. A smile that lit up his whole being and made you feel like you had been given a gift just for seeing it.

Then Derek looked away and went back to his pizza.

Soon, we all relaxed, talking about the regular stuff as Owen and Justin joined us.

"So what's it like on the Elite floor?" Owen asked.

Derek shrugged. "You can look for yourself. It's not like it's off-limits. But you live in a mansion, Price. It's nothing you haven't seen before."

"Just the fact that you've compared it to a mansion makes me curious," I said.

"Fair enough. We have a fifteen-minute break before PE. You should go up and check it out."

I shifted toward Adam. "Want to go? We can..." I trailed off as my eyes flicked over his shoulder. I tensed. "Not again."

"What are you talking about?" asked Adam.

I didn't reply as my gaze locked with Cameron across the cafeteria. Cameron, Santiago, Heath, and seven other guys were weaving around the tables, bearing down on us fast.

"What the fuck is this?!" Cameron cried, making half the table jump. He swooped down and snatched up the pizza box. "What do you think you're doing, Grayson? You can't buy them pizza."

Derek shot to his feet. "What are you? The hall monitor? Why don't you mind your business for once?!"

The shouting was drawing attention. A hush began to fall over the room.

His lips peeled back in a snarl, twisting his beautiful face. "This is my business. Outside food is for *Elites* only. If your F friends want pizza, they need to hop in a time machine, go back to orientation week, and not screw up."

Crash!

Derek's chair toppled over as he shoved away from the table. He stalked up to Cameron, getting in his face. "This is the last time I'm going to say this: you don't tell me what to do. It's my pizza. I'll give it to whoever I want."

Santi stepped forward, wedging himself between them as he gazed at Derek with a look I did not like. The other boys must have seen it too because they jumped to their feet at the same time I did. Although, I don't think it was for the same reason.

"Come on, guys," I snapped. "Are you really going to start a fight over pizza?! Just let it go!"

"There isn't going to be a fight," said a calm voice.

I spun and saw three boys had come up behind me. I had no clue who they were. The three of them had at least a foot on me and stubble on their well-defined jaws. I might have thought they were adults if it wasn't for the E on their chests.

"No one is fighting," repeated the boy in the middle. "But Cameron is right. You can't share privileges, or what is the point of the system? If they want pizza, they battle for it. End of story."

Derek glowered at him. "And you are?"

"Andres," he replied. "And this is Rylan and Greg. We're senior Elites."

"So what? You think I'm afraid of you? I don't have to do a damn thing you say either!"

My eyes ping-ponged between Derek and Andres. I wasn't sure whether to be impressed or annoyed with Derek's ability to piss off every living soul. I've never met anyone else less concerned with making enemies.

Andres laughed. "I can tell you don't scare easily since you're facing down a kid who could snap you in half."

I eyed Santi. Andres wasn't exaggerating. The guy was huge.

"But I'm not threatening you," he continued. "I'm trying to help you. We've been here for years. We know how this goes. Friends get put in different classes and the higher-ups start feeling bad. They share their privileges with their friends, but then the other Ds and Cs get jealous. Why should they have to battle if Derek's giving it away for free? Things get messy. It reaches Argyle and Whittaker and they crack down on all of us.

"Trust me, it's easier on everyone if we all stay in our lane. The next time you have trouble finishing your pie"—he held out his hand and Cameron passed him the box—"your Elite brothers will be happy to help."

With that, the three of them strode off. They were starting in on the pizza before they even sat down.

Cameron and the sophomore Elites backed away, still shooting daggers at us, but their reaction was expected. What wasn't expected were the sideways, semi-satisfied looks from the other boys around us. They hadn't been too impressed with our pizza party either. Andres may have had a point about staying in our lanes.

We finished lunch in a much more subdued mood and then broke apart for our classes. Mr. Dawson welcomed us back and had us open our books and jump in right away.

It was interesting being taught by someone other than Mom. She wasn't one who could stay still, which wasn't surprising considering how often we changed countries. But when she taught me, she used the whole space, striding up and down the room, gesturing with her hands even if there was nothing to point to. She'd often take me out into the city, town, or village and teach me as we explored.

Not at Breakbattle. No one moved from their wobbly seats and Mr. Dawson didn't venture from the area between his desk and the chalkboard. Instead of back-and-forth discussions, Dawson made us sit quietly and only speak when called on. It's not like I thought traditional school life would be glamorous, but seeing it in movies was very different from experiencing it myself.

"Okay, class." Dawson turned away from the board, dusting off his hands. "You were told to pack gym clothes and I hope you heeded that or you'll be running up and down the court in your uniform. Head back to your dorms and get changed."

Everyone stood, said goodbye to Dawson, and headed out. I peeked over my shoulder as we stepped through the doors and saw Tanner and Nico right behind us.

"So are we doing it?" Tanner asked. "Going up to the Elite Wing?"

"Sure," said Adam. "But we have to be quick. Coaches come down hard if you're late. Mom came home ranting once because Coach Singh made a student do fifty suicides and he threw up."

"I don't know what that is and I don't want to find out," I said. "How about we go after basketball?"

"That's a better idea."

The four of us hoofed it to the dorm. Adam went in and immediately started changing, unaware of my averted eyes and warm cheeks, while I pulled out my gym clothes and turned to go back out. "I'll change in the bathroom."

"You can change in here," he said, now down to his boxers. "I don't mind."

"No, it's okay." I hurried out before he could say anything and ducked into the bathroom. My mistake smacked me in the face.

The bathroom was packed with boys in varying states of undress. Boys in boxers. Boys in briefs. Boys lifting their bare arms to slather on deodorant. Boys bending over as they pulled up their shorts. Boys flexing as they took off their shirts. Boys putting their hands on each other as they goofed around.

I stopped dead in the doorway. There was manflesh every-where. What was I supposed to do?

Run!

I darted out of the bathroom. I was halfway down the hall when Adam stepped out of the room, fully dressed.

"Go on ahead," I threw at him. "I'll catch up."

I slipped in behind him, and then slammed and locked the door shut.

"Ohhhkkkayy," I heard through the wood. "See you over there."

I changed in peace and then left for practice. I stepped through the doors just in time and Coach blew his whistle for us to gather up.

"Everyone, grab a seat on the bleachers and we'll get start-ed."

As the lesson got underway, I quickly realized all that stress about changing into my gym clothes was for nothing. I didn't get them sweaty. I didn't so much as move from the bench.

Coach spent the entire lesson teaching us the rules and ba-sics of the game. I shouldn't have been surprised. F kids start at the beginning.

"...that is what we call traveling," said Coach Singh. "An-other important rule of the game: personal fouls. Five of these and you will be removed."

I let my mind wander as he droned on. I knew all the rules from my sports math study sessions during orientation. It was bad enough being denied what the other students have, but we didn't need to be treated like we were clueless on top of it.

"What do you guys think?" Nico asked when we stepped out. "Should we knock out our homework? I wouldn't mind help with the math, Zeke. You really seemed to get that stuff Dawson was talking about."

"Sure, I'll help. Do you guys want to work out here?" I pointed out the other students gathering on the grass. "It's a nice day and better than squeezing into our rooms."

"Sounds good," said Tanner, "but first, the Elite Wing."

"No, first," Adam interrupted, pulling him up short. "We have to change into our uniforms. They're serious about the detentions."

We went back to the dorms, changed, got our backpacks, and then met back up in front of the main building. It was a bit of a weird energy as we slipped inside and turned the corner for the stairs. Even though Derek reminded us we weren't barred from being up here, we were soundless as we climbed to the top.

The double doors that greeted us were nothing like the ones we passed through that morning. These were a light oak with a curlicue E carved into the wood.

Adam was the one to step forward and push open the door. Tanner and Nico darted ahead, rushing inside to see what the fuss was about, while I followed behind at a much slower pace. My jaw dropped when I stepped over the threshold.

Derek said this shouldn't surprise anyone who lived in a mansion, so it felt right for me to be bowled over. Being on the top floor afforded them higher ceilings and this one was lined with chandeliers that cast a gentle glow over the hall. The portraits were back. The faces of men I didn't know but could assume were influential smiled, smirked, or stared seriously at us. Between them were more heavy oak doors with engraved gold nameplates.

This space was night and day to the F Wing. The floors gleamed they were so spotless. There was a water fountain on one end and a vending machine on the other.

"It is nice up here," I said, "but we should go before someone catches us."

Tanner scoffed. "We're not going without seeing the classrooms. Come on." He reached for the door nearest us. "I bet they're insane."

"Tan—!"

He threw it open and ran in. "Whoa," we heard. "This is—Oops."

"Who are you?" another voice said. "What do you think you're doing bursting in here?"

Nico groaned. "Nice job, T."

"Who's out there? All of you, get in here now."

One by one, we marched inside the classroom.

Oh my gosh. How can this be real?

Insane was not the word to describe the room I had walked into. There were *no* words to describe this classroom. The floors in here were not plain white tiles, but a dark hardwood. My eyes rolled around in my head, trying to see everything at once.

I gazed in awe at the back wall. The entire thing was a floor-to-ceiling bookshelf labeled by subject. The desks were arranged in two rows of five and I meant proper desks—with compartments, a keyboard tray, sleek computers, and leather desk chairs.

A woman stood behind a desk that was bigger than the rest. Behind her, there were two whiteboards and in between them was an interactive smartboard displaying the day's work. My eyes narrowed as I focused in on what was written.

"Sorry to burst in, Mrs. Peterson," said Adam. "We just wanted to check out the Elite classrooms."

"Oh, Adam, dear. Is that you?" The woman lost her frown instantly. "I haven't seen you since your parents' Christmas party." She flapped a hand at us. "Come in, come in. You're free to look around."

Tanner and Nico didn't need to be told twice. They went in separate directions, checking out everything.

"It's nice, isn't it?" Peterson said. "I worked at Somerset University before I came here. A fine institution but I've never taught in a classroom quite like this."

I was barely listening. The numbers were whirling in my mind. The problem on the screen was a tricky one. My favorite kind.

I pointed at the marker she was holding. "Can I see that?"

She glanced at me, and then her eyes flicked to the patch on my chest. "Oh no, dear. This is a polynomial. It's from my intro to precalculus lesson. Very advanced and very difficult."

I shrugged. "I don't know. I wouldn't say polynomials are more difficult than matrices. This is only a quadratic equation. Once you know the formula, you're just solving for x."

Peterson blinked. "Excuse me?"

I took the marker from her limp fingers and descended on the whiteboard. The room was silent as my hand flashed across the board. It was almost keeping in time with my mind.

"There," I said after writing the final number. "The answer is the square root of eleven plus two." I stepped back and shot Mrs. Peterson's gaping surprise a smile. "Do you have another one I can do? I love quadratic equations."

"Who... are you?"

"Oh. I'm sorry. My name is Zeke Manning." I held out my hand. "Nice to meet you."

She made no move to take it. "I'm afraid I don't understand."

"Don't understand why this guy has an F on his chest?" Adam piped up. "It's a long story that resulted in both of us missing the placement test."

She gasped. "I did hear of that, but I didn't know that was you, Adam." She turned on me, looking at me in a new light. "And you, Zeke, should clearly not be in that class. Solving polynomials as a freshman. What was Principal Whittaker thinking? You should have been allowed a retake."

I shook my head. "It's okay. There's nothing I can do about it except decide if I'll participate in the tournament."

"It's not okay. It's near enough to a crime to let a strong young mind like yours stagnate. F students don't take pre-calculous until their senior year."

My shoulders slumped. "I know. My teacher told me that today."

She tossed her head. It was obvious she was genuinely bothered by our situation. "There must be something— Wait. I have an idea." She turned and opened her drawer.

"An idea?"

After a few seconds, she made a pleased noise and righted herself. Peterson faced me with a triumphant smile. In her hand was a single sheet of paper. "The Archimedean Club. This is the math club I run after school. From what I've seen, you'll be a great fit."

"I've heard of this," I admitted as I took the flyer. "I'd love to join but it says right here it's for Bs and up."

"Yes, but that needn't stop you. The way it works is the first fifteen students who sign up from those three classes are guaranteed a spot and then, if anyone else wants to join, they have to battle one of them for it. So that's what you'll do.

"Club teams are one of the rare exceptions to the battle rules, because once a member loses their spot, they lose it for the entire semester. We participate in competitions so it's no good for a team for the members to change constantly. Once I finalize the roster, that's it. So make sure you're on it."

"That's— That's perfect," I breathed. "Thank you so much, Mrs. Peterson."

"Of course. Now, if you were serious about answering more problems, I was prepping this lesson for my class tomorrow."

I beamed, practically bouncing on my heels. "I was very serious."

"Wonderful." She glanced at Adam, Tanner, and Nico. "You boys probably have homework, so why don't you get a jump on it? You can sit at the desk, but I can't allow you on the computers."

They easily took her up on her offer. The three of them pulled up chairs and gathered around a desk to work. It wasn't much. Just an algebra worksheet and a small essay. I would be able to knock that out after dinner. In the meantime, I was having way more fun with Mrs. Peterson. Not for the first time I felt the twinge of not getting into the Elite Class. Mr. Dawson was a nice man, but I was learning more since I walked into this classroom than I had all day.

"A great way to remember the quadratic equation is to sing it to the tune of *Pop Goes the Weasel*. Trust me, you'll never forget it."

I laughed. "Really? Wow. I never learned that trick."

"Why don't you try this one?" She went up to the board and wrote out another problem. "It's a little tricky. Hint: the answer can be negative or positive."

"Okay." I took her place. "So when do you start functions?" I asked as I worked. "That's where my mom and I left off."

"I hope to touch on it later in the semester with my class, but it's on the curriculum for the Archimedean Club as well."

Knock. Knock.

I heard the door open behind us.

"Faith? Have you finished the field trip proposal? I want to see— Hello? Who are you boys?"

"I'm Adam."

"Tanner."

"Nico."

"Charmed, gentlemen," the man said slowly. "But I know all of our Elite boys and I'm certain you three aren't one of them."

My hand stilled. Something in his voice made me face him. The man that entered looked smart in his neat brown suit and polished shoes. I couldn't give the same compliment to his downturned lips or the obvious wrinkle between his brows.

"What class are you in?"

Adam lifted his chin. "We're in the F Class."

"Excuse me? What are you doing in here?"

Mrs. Peterson stepped around her desk. "Arthur, I invited them to stay. Now, my proposal is on my desk. You can—"

"I'm sorry. What do you mean you've invited them to stay?" The man advanced on her. "You know as well as I do that they aren't allowed to use these materials or Elite resources. As no battles have been won or lost yet, there is no feasible reason they should be in here."

His voice rose as his speech went on. Looking past him, I made eye contact with Adam. I couldn't see my expression but it had to be at least twice as uncomfortable as his.

"Mr. Orlov," Mrs. Peterson said in a low voice. "Kindly calm down."

"I am calm, Faith, considering the circumstances. They should not be at our student's desk and he should be nowhere near the smartboard."

I stiffened when his beady eyes turned on me.

"These materials are very expensive and for our students' use only. What if they had broken or damaged something?"

"For heaven's sake, they're not toddlers. I've told you already they are not using the materials. The others are simply sitting at the desk doing their homework and Zeke has not touched the smartboard. He is working on the whiteboard only."

"Why would he be doing that? He can't answer that problem."

I bristled. "Yes, I can."

"He can," Peterson echoed. "He is one of the freshmen that missed the placement test. It turns out he's quite gifted."

"Gifted, is he? But evidently not concerned about being responsible or carrying out his duties. Yes, I heard about this supposed death prank that resulted in two of our best students receiving detention, but they tell a very different story than the one I've heard."

"What?" I broke in. "What did they say?"

He finally looked at me. "Apparently, you took a dislike to your group leaders and lured them out into the woods to play a prank on them. When it went wrong and you missed the test, you told the vice principal it was the other way around."

"That's a lie!"

Bright spots of color appeared on his cheeks. "I beg your pardon. Do not speak to me in that tone! Cameron Dupre and Santiago Holland are Elite. They have been model students since they have set foot on this campus. I have every reason to believe their version of events."

He twisted to the side and pointed at the door. "Your homework can be done in your own classroom with your own desks and boards. Leave immediately."

I clenched the marker so tightly my fingers sang out for blood. I had met all kinds of people in my life, but never had I been outright dismissed like I was little more than trash.

Stiffly, I stepped away from the board. The other guys were already packing away their things.

"I'm very sorry, boys," said Peterson. To her credit, she was glaring hard at her colleague. "You should go as I do have work I need to get to, but I don't want you to think you're unwelcome here. You four are not barred from any part of this campus."

Arthur sniffed. "That may be the case, but the smart thing for everyone to do is stay where they belong. I don't expect I'll see you boys up here again."

Maybe I shouldn't have, but those hideous words drilled into my soul, judging me when I hadn't done a single thing wrong. I paused at the exit and looked him straight in the eye.

"I wouldn't count on it."

The door slammed on him mid-sputter.

"THAT WAS SERIOUSLY cool," Adam gushed. "I'm pretty sure that guy hates you, if he didn't already, but still it was cool."

I laughed as I packed my backpack for the next day. After getting kicked out of the Elite Wing, the four of us went outside to finish working. It took a while since they alternated from cursing out Orlov to praising me for standing up to him. Now Adam and I were back in the dorm getting ready for dinner.

"I guess this means you've decided to do the tournament."

Sighing, I heaved myself out of my chair. "No, I haven't. I don't have a problem with not getting pizzas or parties or working with computers and smartboards. My mom and I used to have lessons on park benches, I know you can learn without those things. But what does bother me is taking classes that are too easy for me."

I glanced away as Derek's face floated in my mind. "There are a lot of reasons I need to be in this school, but my education is important to me."

"So what's the problem?"

"The problem is we all feel that way. Everyone is pushing themselves hard in this weird school to hang on to what they have. How am I supposed to feel right about ripping someone out of the A or Elite Class and making them an F. It could send their whole future off track."

My heart squeezed as an uncomfortable thought occurred to me. "And that's what happened to Becca Taylor, isn't it? They ran her into the ground and then challenged her to a tournament."

"Yes," Adam said softly. "That's what happened."

"How can I do that to someone else?"

He put up his hands. "Hold on. You wouldn't be. Becca was targeted and bullied by vicious assholes, and *you* lost your chance to be in the right class also because of vicious assholes. To be honest, it doesn't matter what class I'm in because I'll take over my father's company either way. Can you say the same thing? Your future is important too, Zeke."

I lowered my head, jaw clenching. Right now, nothing mattered more than getting close to Derek, but I had done the hard part. He was beginning to see me as a friend and soon he would open up to me completely. When that was done, I would make right everything that happened to me and finally chase the voices away.

But after this was over, I would still need to get into a good college and get a decent job. There were no companies waiting for me to take over. I needed to move classes. I just didn't want to sacrifice an innocent kid to do it.

"This is another lesson they want us to learn, isn't it?" I whispered. "That to get what we want in life, sometimes we have to step on a few heads to climb to the top."

"I don't think it'd make you feel better if I said yes." Adam crossed the room and threw his arm around my shoulder. "Don't worry about it now. You have the whole year to decide what you want to do, but know that I've got your back either way."

I smiled. It was a tiny one, but still, it was a smile. "Thanks. You're a good friend."

"Let's go eat. I'm starved."

I didn't need more prompting. We headed down to the cafeteria and hopped on the food line. We picked up oven-fried chicken, rice, beans, corn, a choice of fruit, and a chocolate cookie.

We took it to an empty table and sat down. Derek may have hated it, but I didn't mind the food. I could tell it was cooked fresh instead of frozen, reheated, and stuck under a hot plate. That was good enough for me.

I cut off a slice of chicken and brought it to my lips.

"Hey, guys." A tray dropped down in front of me. "How was your summer?"

My eyes popped. Slipping through my fingers, the fork clattered to my plate as I gazed at her. "Oh my goodness, Melody? How?" I leveled a finger at her chest. "What are you doing with that?"

She groaned as she looked down at the E on her patch. "I know. It's awful. It makes me look like such a hypocrite after everything I said over orientation week. The other girls have been letting me have it and I can't blame them. It was a hard choice, but I don't believe a girl should ever dumb herself down. Purposely flunking felt too wrong." She glanced between us, genuinely looking upset. "You understand, don't you?"

Adam nodded. "Of course, I do. You're smart and talented. You should never pretend otherwise. Besides, your class doesn't have to stop you from fighting."

She beamed. "Thank you, Adam." Melody reached across the table and curled her fingers over his hand. "You're so sweet."

I hid a smile at his stiffening body. Melody had touched him. His mind would be on vacation for at least an hour.

She shifted toward me and leaned forward. Her beautiful face was fixed in the most serious expression. "Adam is right. I want you to know that nothing has changed. I'm still committed to fighting the system no matter what class I'm in. If anything, I'm in an even better position to do it because I have all the privileges and I can get in everywhere. Tomorrow, I'm meeting with Mrs. Argyle and asking her to let me form a student organization for all classes and *both* campuses."

"Will she go for that?"

She winked. "It's all in how you present it, Zeke."

"Good luck. Tell me if there's anything I can do."

"I will." She took her tray and got to her feet. "I'm going to find my friends. See you guys tomorrow."

Owen and Justin came up just as she walked away. I looked over their heads for Derek.

Where is he?

My question was answered almost immediately. Derek was sitting near the front table, sandwiched between two girls, and I meant sandwiched. They were draped all over him, snuggling into his side.

Apparently, he can make friends.

I looked away as my fists balled under the table. He never said he'd sit with me all the time, but it was hard enough getting to spend time with him when we were in different classes. How was I supposed to get close to him if we didn't talk or hang out?

Someone crossed in front of my vision, blocking out Derek. I traveled up his blazer and connected with bright green orbs.

Landon Foster.

I held still. No clue why. It wasn't like not moving would make him unsee me. Either way, I couldn't move if I wanted to. Landon was looking at me... and he was coming this way.

He stopped behind Owen and Justin. "Hey, guys. Mind if I sit?"

I opened my mouth. "I—"

"Sure," Owen said. "It's cool with us."

Landon thanked him and moved around the table. He kept his eyes on me as he pulled out the chair by my side and sat down.

"Zeke."

I swallowed hard. My heart was thumping wildly against my chest. Landon looked so good. Being forced out of the designer clothes and into the uniform should have made him into a mere mortal like the rest of us, but somehow, he made the other boys look like they were wearing burlap sacks.

I bet he'd even look good in that sack.

I squeezed my eyes shut as that never-to-be-voiced thought went through my head. If I was wondering if I still had a crush on him, there was my answer. But feelings aside, there was one problem.

"What are you doing here, Landon?"

"You know why I'm here."

Sighing, I opened my eyes and looked at him. I knew Landon, Cole, and Michael were pissed about orientation week, but I had done the right thing. He could chew me out if he wanted to, I wouldn't back down.

"Go on, then," I said. "Let's hear it."

"I'm sorry."

"I didn't do—" I stopped.

What did he just say?

"What was that?" I asked.

"I'm sorry for how things went down over orientation. You never should have missed the test. I felt bad when I heard you were busted down to F. You're a human calculator. You don't belong in that class."

"I wouldn't say I'm a human calculator," I replied. Then I flushed.

Seriously, Zela. That's the part of his speech you want to focus on?

"I can't believe you're apologizing," I continued. "I thought you were mad at me."

He screwed up his face. "What? Why would I be mad at you? You weren't behind that sick shit with Derek."

"I know, but you didn't talk to me after it happened."

Landon peered around, then he leaned in. "It wasn't because I was mad at you."

He was so close I could count the gold flecks in his contacts.

"I was mad at myself," he whispered. "It was wrong walking away with Cameron. I was so messed up I threw up before I went into the test. All I could see was him lying there. I didn't know what I was going to do until seconds before I walked in the room. I was going to tell Argyle the truth but—"

"But Derek was there," I finished. "Alive and well."

He lowered his head. "Yeah. I figured out pretty quickly that was the real test to get into the Network. I should have backed you up with Argyle but Cameron made it clear what they would do to us if we did. If it makes you feel any better, Cole did get in a solid punch before Santi stepped in."

I cracked a smile. "I don't like violence, but it's nice to know you guys aren't siding with them. Thanks, Landon."

There weren't words to describe how relieved I was. My crush could go nowhere while I was pretending to be Zeke, but there was a brief moment where I thought we were becoming friends and I wanted that. I wanted to give him my apples, sit together at lunch, do math homework together. Whatever kept me near this sweet-smelling, raven-haired Adonis.

Nodding, he leaned back. "I am sorry and I'm not on Cameron's side. He's a dick and I never liked him." He clapped a hand on my shoulder. "So know that I don't have a choice."

My smile twitched. "A choice about what? What are you talking about?"

Landon's hand slipped off me as he pushed back his chair. "This."

I looked up at him in confusion as he cleared his throat.

"Zeke Manning," he said clearly. "I challenge you to a battle."

Chapter Three

“**A** battle?!” I cried.

"Did you hear that?" someone said. "I think he said battle."

"He definitely did," replied a voice closer to us. "First challenge of the year."

"What the hell are you doing?" This came from Adam.

Landon didn't look away from me. "I'm challenging you to a battle. We can make it official in the morning."

He turned his back.

"Wait. A battle for what? Why are you doing this?!" I shouted at him, but he didn't slow down. He walked out of the cafeteria while I sat too stunned to move.

Someone grabbed my arm and turned me around. "Zeke, what was he saying to you?"

It took me a second to register Adam's question. "He said he was sorry and then he just..."

"I don't get it," Justin said. "Why would he challenge you? Landon has all of the privileges and you have none. What would the battle be over?"

I didn't have an answer to that. I didn't have answers for any of their questions and soon they gave up and went back to their food, casting odd looks at me as they ate.

What was I supposed to think? Landon apologizes and then challenges me to a battle after cryptically saying he has no choice. No matter which way I looked at it, that did not sound like a good thing, but Owen was right. What would we battle over when I had nothing for him to take?

My mind was a tangle of questions and conflicting emotions as we left the dining room and returned to our dorm.

"Everything is going to be fine, Zeke," Adam spoke up from his bed. "If something is up, we'll figure it out and stop it."

I burrowed down and pulled the sheets up to my chin. "Thanks, Adam. I know we will."

He gave me a smile before shutting off the light. I forced myself to close my eyes, but it was hours before I got my mind to slow enough for sleep to catch me.

The next morning, I woke early, showered, and came in as Adam was waking up.

I sat on my bed to wait for him. When he came back from the shower, he finished getting ready and we picked up our backpacks to go. Adam pulled open the door.

Landon stood with his fist aloft, moments away from knocking. "Manning, you're ready. Good. We need to hurry before class starts."

I gaped at him. "How... did you know this was my dorm?"

Seriously, Zela?! That's your first question?! How is that important right now?

"What I meant was what are you doing?" I said quickly. "Why are you challenging me, Landon? I have nothing. I have *less* than nothing."

"You don't think I know that?" He stepped back. "Let's go, Zeke. We have to find our teachers and make it official. Unless you're refusing and willing to lose ten points off your final grade."

My grip tightened on my backpack strap. "Of course, I'm not."

"Then to the Elite Wing we go."

He strode off, knowing I would follow.

Stifling a curse, I hurried after him. The footsteps behind me said Adam was coming along. "Tell me what's going on right now."

"You haven't figured it out yet?"

He got ahead of me as he pushed through the door. I practically ran after him.

"You said you had no choice. This is Cameron, isn't it?" I stared hard at the side of his face. "He told you to battle me."

"Yep." I caught his frown. "Everyone says the Elite rarely get challenged. No one even wants to try, but that dick has me battling my first week of school."

"Why?"

He scoffed. "You think he shares his plans with me? All I know is I've got orders."

"Orders?" My hand shot out and grabbed him. Digging in my heels, I spun him around and made him stop. "From Cameron? Who is he to give you orders? Why don't you tell him to shove it?"

"Dammit, Zeke!" Looking at him head on, I could see the emotions warring on his face. "You don't think I want to? I'm in now and if I want to stay in, I do what he says. Cameron made that very clear."

He closed his eyes and took a breath. "Look, it's just one battle, and like you said, you have nothing to lose. Let's get it over with."

It's not just one battle. I don't have to ask what he means by being in now. Cameron's playing some kind of game and going along with this will draw me in.

It's not like I have a choice, another voice countered. *Refusing the battle means my grade takes a hit and I'm sure Cameron will be just as happy with me flunking out.*

"Fine," I said. "Let's get it over with."

"Good." Landon cut eyes to Adam. "You don't need to come."

"I'm not going anywhere."

He shrugged. "Suit yourself."

Landon took off again and we followed him out to the main building and up the stairs. The Elite Wing was just as magnificent as I remembered, but this time it was filled with boys. They gathered in groups, talking and laughing with their friends. They looked no different from the other guys in the school, but I don't believe they had the same thought as they turned and saw me and Adam. Conversation ceased at the sight of our patches.

"What's this?" Andres peeled himself off the wall. The older boy stepped out in front of us, walking backwards as he sized us up. "Brought us a visitor, Foster?"

"It's battle business," he replied.

Andres's brows shot up his head. "Are you kidding? *He* challenged you to a battle? In what? Art?"

That kicked off a round of laughter that made me scowl. I got it. The only thing an F kid could beat an Elite at was doodling. I was starting to get real tired of these people underestimating me.

"No," Landon said over their noise. "I challenged him."

Andres lost his grin. "You what? Why would you do that?"

The guy had clearly missed the show last night. I'd be annoyed but part of me was enjoying the dumbfounded look on his face.

"We need to go," said Landon.

Andres stepped aside, but I felt his eyes on me as we passed.

Landon led us to an open door at the end of the hall. "Sir?" he said as he stepped in. "I need you to approve a battle."

"So soon? The A students can be quite overeager."

I tensed at the sound of that voice. I knew before I walked in and saw him standing before his precious smartboard that it was—

"Mr. Orlov."

"You?" His forehead squished into half a dozen rows of wrinkles. "What did I tell you? I will not stand for your disrespect. Leave this—"

"Sir," Landon interrupted. "He's my opponent."

If anything, the man got redder. "You dare waste my student's time with a nonsense challenge!"

"I challenged him."

He cut off mid-rant. "You did what?"

Goodness. Was everyone going to have that reaction?

Landon crossed the room and stepped up to his teacher's desk. They devolved into what looked to be a heated discussion while Adam and I hung back at the door.

I met the eyes of the other boys in the room. When we came in, Michael and Cole were leaning against one of the desks, looking at Michael's phone. Now they were staring at us.

"My mom said she worked with a pretentious asshole that drove her nuts," Adam whispered out of the corner of his mouth. "I don't know about you, but I have a tiny feeling it's Orlov."

I laughed under my breath. "You know, I think you're on to something. But give him a minute, I think he's just getting started."

We busted up, fighting hard not to make noise. This was so not the time to be laughing, but Orlov's face when I walked inside was priceless. Like I was a ticking unmarked package instead of a harmless fifteen-year-old. Why did he care so much if Fs were up here? He didn't own the place.

On the other side of the room, Zach turned away from his computer. "Hey, Adam. How was your summer?"

Adam's chuckles dried up so fast it was like a switch flipped. Slowly, he turned his back on Zachary. "I'll wait for you outside, Zeke."

I watched Zach as his former best friend walked out on him. Something flickered across his face—too fast for me to make it out, then it was gone.

"All right. You have my approval." I took my attention off him as Orlov stepped around his desk. "Gentlemen, I suspect I will be late to class. I want you all to start the reading I assigned for this week. I trust you'll behave yourself in a manner befitting your class until I return."

"Umm." I looked from Orlov to Landon. "We're going to speak to my teacher now, right? Do you need to come with us?"

"I do indeed." Orlov smiled. "I suspect there will be an issue, so I will come along to smooth it out. This battle will go ahead. I'll ensure it."

My stomach had been in knots since Landon made his challenge, thinking of every possible motive behind this move. Seeing Mr. Orlov smile twisted it up even tighter.

Silently, the three of us trailed him out of the Elite Wing, down the stairs, and through the doors of the F hallway. Mr. Dawson got to his feet when we walked in.

"Arthur? What's going on? I thought we settled this yesterday. My students are free to be in the Elite Wing as long as they aren't causing a disturbance."

I shot an incredulous look at the back of Orlov's head. The man complained about us? Seriously?

The class was almost full. Boys were talking, laughing, throwing their backpacks down, and scraping their chairs across the floor, but the noise died down as Orlov spoke.

"That is not why I'm here, Sandy." He gestured at me and Landon. "My student has challenged yours to a battle. He has chosen history and once your student chooses the physical test, you can approve it. We'll speak to the proper coach today and set a time. It's the first week, so battle schedules are clear. I don't think we'll have an issue setting it for tomorrow."

Mr. Dawson put his hand up. "Whoa, whoa, whoa. Did you say your student has challenged mine? For what? Zeke has no privileges."

"Ah, that is true. But Mr. Foster has made me aware of an interesting fact about the rules." He grasped Landon's shoulder, smiling away. "Zeke does not have privileges, but he does have... a chair."

"A chair?" Adam, Dawson, and I said at the same time.

"What chair?" I asked.

Orlov turned to me. "Students saw you move a chair into your dorm yesterday. The battle will be held over that item."

I could not have heard that correctly. "A battle for my chair? Why in the world do you want that, Landon? Doesn't your dorm have a chair? Doesn't it have a whole couch?"

Orlov held up a finger. "The why is not important. The chair is what he has named. Now, tell us what sport you've chosen. Sandy, get the forms."

Dawson sputtered. "I'm not getting any forms! This is ridiculous. Students don't battle over furniture. They do so over privileges, which Zeke *does not* have. You can't think I'll approve this battle."

"You will do so," Orlov said firmly. "This challenge is within the rules and Principal Whittaker will agree with me on this."

"I very much doubt that, but I'm happy to take the matter to him." Dawson snatched up his coat and marched toward the door. "Adam, you stay here. You're in charge of the class until I come back. Your English worksheets are on my desk."

Adam watched us go with wide eyes, clearly just as baffled as me. What in the slippery flipping hell was going on? A battle for a chair? A trip to the principal's office? Was any of this supposed to make sense?

"Are you going to tell me why you want my chair?" I asked Landon as we followed our teachers. They were walking ahead of us, arguing in low tones.

"I would if I knew."

I couldn't be sure, but he sounded sincere. I held back the rest of my questions. It wasn't him I needed to confront.

The four of us left the class wings and headed to the part of the building that held the administration offices. I had never been in Principal Whittaker's office. From what I had seen on television, seeing the inside of a principal's office was a bad thing. It meant you were in trouble.

A short, tidy man in a plaid shirt rose from his seat when we entered. The plate on his desk read Simon Dewan. "Is there a problem?"

"We need to speak to Principal Whittaker," said Dawson. "Mr. Orlov and I are having a disagreement on our interpretation of the rules of battle. Is he available?"

"He is. I'll see if he'll speak with you."

We stood in awkward silence as Dewan spoke to the principal. Or at least, it was awkward for me.

"Yes, sir. That is what he said. A disagreement about the rules. Yes. Yes. As you wish." Dewan set the phone on its cradle. "You may go in."

The teachers led the way to a frosted glass door at the back of the room. Stepping inside was like entering a new world—like leaving an F classroom and walking in an Elite. The plain white walls, beige tile, and standard office equipment hadn't spread into this space.

My soles were swallowed by soft, reddish-brown carpet. It was a nice match for the elegant red damask wallpaper that was covered up by—

I squinted for a better look. *Whittaker.*

It was all Whittaker from framed diplomas, plaques, and photos of him. Photos of him shaking hands with people I had only seen on television, to holding up massive dead fishes, to just him smiling at the camera and proving he also excelled at being handsome. The whole room was a celebration of his achievements.

"Good morning, gentlemen." He didn't rise from his desk. "As you know, I normally reserve the afternoons for handling student issues, but I'm intrigued. Mr. Dewan tells me there is an issue understanding the rules for battle. How can that be? We have operated under these rules for years."

Dawson stepped forward. "It's simple, sir. Arthur's student has challenged mine to a battle, but Zeke has no privileges. Instead, they propose to battle for a chair Zeke purchased for his dorm room. Arthur is trying to make the case that personal items can be used in this case, but I'm sure you will agree, sir, that the rules forbid this."

"A chair?" Whittaker repeated. He zeroed in on me and Landon. "An Elite student has issued a challenge to an F for... a chair?"

"Do you see, sir?" Dawson said "It's ridiculous."

"It's not ridiculous," Orlov said. "It's the only option left for the very reason that F students have no privileges."

Whittaker leaned back in his seat, folding his hands under the desk. "Explain."

"The rules clearly state that battles cannot be held for money or as a means to harm. Personal items are not expressly mentioned. You would agree with that, sir, yes?"

I flicked from Orlov to the principal. His expression was unreadable as he looked back at us. He could have been thinking over Orlov's words, or his summer vacation in Aruba for all he gave away.

After a solid minute, he nodded. "Yes. I would agree with that."

"Would you also agree that the dorms and the way they are set up are included in the privilege system?" Orlov continued. "The F students are entitled to a bed and a trunk while the Elite have desks, sofas, television stands, and wardrobes. The added décor is a reward for their class which makes furniture undoubtedly a part of the system."

Whittaker inclined his head. "This is correct."

"Thank you, sir." Orlov was gaining steam and the smirk on his face said he knew it. "Could the argument not be made that by buying his own chair, Zeke awarded himself a privilege meant for the upper classes?"

"You could make that argument, yes."

I blinked. Wait. What was happening here? Awarded myself a privilege? It was just a stinking chair!

"And one more point, sir." Orlov turned on Dawson. "I find my colleague's insistence on rejecting this battle on the basis of F students having no privileges to be quite disturbing."

Dawson started. "Excuse me?"

"This would set a precedent," he plowed on. "We would be saying that F students should not be challenged *at all* except for when they manage to win a privilege off another. They would be allowed to coast through school, only opting into the system when they feel like it when we both would agree it is the F students who need this system the most."

I jerked when he leveled a finger at me. "Of course, a student cannot take what the other does not have, but as personal items, and *F students*, are not excluded from our system; there is no reason Zeke cannot go to battle for a chair he is not entitled to in the first place."

Dawson spun to face Whittaker. "Sir, you cannot be considering this? Think of the precedent that would set! Items that parents buy for their children are not a part of the system and for good reason."

I nodded along. *Yes, thank you. Tell him how nuts this is. Whatever Cameron is up to, put a stop to it now.*

"We cannot allow students to basically steal from each other," Dawson stated.

Whittaker's expression hadn't changed for the entire conversation. "I've heard your arguments and you both make excellent points, but in this, I must agree with Mr. Orlov."

"But, sir!" I exploded.

Whittaker raised his palm, effectively silencing me. "I'm afraid he's right. F students are most certainly not excluded from being challenged and to deny this battle would be grossly unfair to Ds and up who must be ready at all times to defend their privileges."

I pushed through Orlov and Dawson to plant myself in front of him. "But my mother bought it for me. He can't just take it."

He spread out his hands in an elegant imitation of a shrug. "He won't take it if you win the battle. Besides, the faculty takes personal items from students all the time. Last year alone, I confiscated five gaming systems, two Swiss army knives, more makeup than you can count, and a tuba of all things. That their parents bought it for them made no difference."

"But, sir." Dawson stepped to my side. "There is a difference between the faculty confiscating items that are dangerous or disruptive, and a student picking and choosing what they want to fleece from their classmates."

To my relief, he inclined his head. "Indeed. I can't deny there is an opportunity for abuse so I will let this go ahead with a few caveats. One, the standard one-at-a-time rules apply."

My heart sank as he held up a second finger. He was really doing this. Whittaker was approving this madness.

"Two, items necessary for learning and schoolwork are not eligible. Three, nothing valued at fifty dollars or more is eligible. Four, if the item is not won back in a battle, it must be returned to them at the end of the year with instructions not to bring it back to school. We do this with all confiscated items, so this should head off any complaints that we're allowing students to steal from each other. This is my decision. Is it understood?"

"Yes, sir," Orlov said immediately.

Dawson's reply came slower. A vein throbbed hard in his forehead as he said, "I understand, Principal Whittaker."

"Excellent. Then I'll have Mr. Dewan update the handbooks and send out a document to all the teachers. This battle will proceed with my approval after students and faculty have read and signed that they accept the new rules. I expect this will be done no later than tomorrow."

"Perfect," Orlov replied. "Zeke needs only to choose the physical test and we can get it scheduled this week."

Whittaker nodded. "What have you chosen, Zeke?"

My throat was dry. I tried swallowing multiple times before forcing out, "Soccer. I choose soccer."

"Soccer it is." Finally, Whittaker rose from his chair. "Thank you for bringing this to my attention. I have no doubt it will be for everyone's benefit, but largely I am excited for the impact this will have on our F students. It is them that need the push to fight and persevere that the battle system encourages. I look forward to watching this play out over the semester. If it goes well, I will consider more ways we can shift the system to become more than just a fight for privileges."

I stared at him, lips pressed so tightly I was sure they were going white. He thought this was a good thing? Finding ways for students who were ranked higher to go after students that were already denied privileges. Now it was open season on the things they had to make things bearable at Breakbattle.

Whittaker's lips peeled back in the same charming smile beaming down at us from a dozen photographs. "Goodbye, gentlemen."

Dawson put his hand on my shoulder and gently pulled me away.

It's a chair, I thought as we made the silent march back to class. *It's just a chair.*

Over and over again, I repeated that thought to myself but it was hard to hear over Cameron's whispered taunt echoing in my mind.

"Don't think this is the end. I've got more planned for you snitches."

This was about so much more than a chair.

"THE MAN IS CRAZY. I said he was crazy, didn't I? Him and all the other principals who took over and didn't dump this crap-ass system!" Tanner belted.

Our little group was trailing behind our class. We were on our way to the pool after minutes ago receiving the note from the principal stating the new changes to the system. Mr. Dawson passed them out with a scowl he didn't bother to hide and told us to return them tomorrow morning signed.

Tanner practically ripped it out of his hands and stormed out of the classroom. His rant was going full steam before we caught up to him.

"Like it's not bad enough for us! We can't go in the library, on field trips, join clubs, go to events, or anything. That wasn't fucking bad enough!? No, now our stuff is up for grabs too."

"You can't battle for anything more than fifty dollars," Adam offered. "That's something at least."

Tanner spun on him so fast we almost collided. He got in Adam's face, nostrils flaring. "Fifty dollars is a lot of money to some of us, Moon! Maybe your parents can buy a hundred more of whatever they take, but mine can't!"

I jumped in. "Hey! He didn't mean—"

Adam put a hand on my arm without looking away from Tanner's flashing eyes. "You're right," he said calmly. "I shouldn't have said that."

Tanner stared him down for a few more tense seconds. Then his shoulders relaxed. "Nah. I'm sorry," he said as he backed away. "I'm not pissed at you. I'm mad at Whittaker.

And maybe you're right, they can't battle for my laptop or"—he glanced down at his wrist—"my grandpa's watch, so who would bother?"

"For sure, T," Nico spoke up. "We didn't pack anything special. Nothing that everyone here doesn't already have. I think we'll be fine."

"You guys will be fine," I stated. "I know you will."

Because this is not about you.

The four of us dropped the conversation as we headed into the natatorium as Mr. Dawson called it, or the indoor swimming pool.

"All right, boys." A man emerged from the locker room in neon orange swim trunks, a white tank, and black aqua shoes. Coach Nelson should have looked funny in that outfit, but somehow it suited him. The guy was one big muscle with a strong jaw and powerful limbs to cut through the water. He probably came out the womb in trunks. "Take a seat and listen up."

We did as ordered and filed onto the stands. Adam elbowed me as we sat down. "When will you talk to Nelson?"

I hitched my backpack up my shoulder. "I'll talk to him after this."

"Welcome," Nelson began. "We will talk briefly about what I expect this semester and going forward. This period will be broken into blocks of three for beginner, intermediate, and expert. I have chosen your placement based on your scores on the trials and I will not change my mind, so do not ask. After your block has ended, you are free to leave."

He pointed over his shoulder. "There is a reason you were told not to bring swimsuits. Suits were purchased for you using your measurements for the uniforms. They are new and waiting for you in the locker. Expert block is first up. I'll call your names. You guys head back and get changed."

It came as no surprise when Adam was first to be called for expert block. He and five other guys in my class stood and headed for the lockers.

"The rest of you stay here and keep the noise down."

I stood when Nelson turned to go. Hurrying down the steps, I jogged past the serene crystal blue pool to catch up with him. "Excuse me, Coach Nelson."

"Yes?" He didn't stop walking.

"I need to speak with you."

"I'm listening."

"It's about..." My eyes bugged when I noticed what door he was heading for.

"Coach, if you could just—"

Nelson pushed open the boys' locker room.

"I can't go in—!"

"One more thing," Nelson called to the boys. "There are swim caps in that box." The door swung closed behind him.

I jerked to a stop; my feet stuck to the floor like it was quicksand. The little sign of a man stared back, mocking me and the one hurdle I wouldn't be able to fake my way through.

The door swung open. "Manning, get in here," Nelson demanded. "I'm about to start class. You have something to say, now is your time."

I gulped. "Could we... speak out here?"

He frowned. "What? Is this important or not?"

Sighing, I took a step over the threshold. Moving so fast the room and nude bodies blurred, I jumped out in front of him and turned my back so all I could see was Nelson and the door.

His frown was going full force as he crossed his arms. "I'm assuming this is about you not being able to swim? Well, let me tell you now you still have to participate. You'll be in the beginner group and you'll learn the basics. Your only other option is a zero for this class."

"It's not about that, Coach. I wanted to speak with you about the swimsuits." I shrugged my backpack off and unzipped it. "I can't wear the one the school provides."

"And why is that?"

"It's my belief," I stated clearly. "I can't be exposed in front of people and being in only trunks is too revealing."

"What the hell?" someone said. "Is this guy for real?"

Coach snapped his head up. "Quiet, Park. I told you to get dressed." I held still as he returned his attention to me. "Your belief, you say?"

I nodded. I knew the implication he was drawing and even though it felt dishonest to let him think it, it was absolutely true that I did not believe in stripping in the middle of a room full of guys. I wouldn't have been comfortable around girls either, but in this case, I had to do something. Mom and I went back and forth on it for a week and this is what we agreed. She was even ready to back me up if I put Nelson on the phone.

I pulled it out. It was a full-body wetsuit. The suit also covered my head so there was no chance of my wig coming off in the water. "This will cover my body and it matches the color and style of the school suits. Will this be okay, Coach?"

I read that traditional schools had to respect their students' beliefs but I didn't know how far that went, especially in a strict place like Breakbattle.

He took the suit from me, eyeing it curiously. "Hmm. It does match our suits. I appreciate the trouble you went through to find this." He handed it back. "Breakbattle is respectful of all their students and their beliefs. This suit would not be allowed if you were on the swim team, but I'm assuming you have no intention of joining?"

I shook my head.

"Then it shouldn't be a problem. As for getting changed, you can do so after the others have left the locker room."

I was so relieved I thought I might cry. I braced myself for way more arguing and maybe another trip to Whittaker. Thank goodness one thing had gone right for me since I set foot on this campus.

I scurried out and practice got underway. The beginner block was at the very end, so as agreed, I went into the locker room after the others were dressed, changed quickly, and then hopped in the pool for Nelson to teach me how to hold my breath underwater and float. Not an exciting lesson, but I skipped back to the dorm feeling confident. I was kicking butt at being Zeke. Nothing Cameron could throw at me would be harder than navigating locker rooms.

Adam was in our room working on homework when I came in long after everyone else. I pulled out my stuff and we worked on it together until dinner.

Owen and Justin had beat us to the cafeteria and snagged our favorite table. This time it wasn't just the two of them.

We sat down and they introduced us to their new friends from the C and B Class. I took a minute to look around for Derek, and found him at a table surrounded by girls again.

This isn't going to work, I thought as I eyed him. *I have to be more proactive.*

"Hey, Melody."

The name made me tear my eyes off him. Melody smiled broadly as she came up to our table. Clutched to her chest was a clipboard. "Mind if I join you?"

She was pulling out the chair before Adam could get out a yes. "Zeke. Adam. Guess what?" She spun the clipboard around. "I got Argyle to approve the organization!"

"You did?" I said. "What magic did you pull to get her to agree to an organization against the school?"

She smirked. "Simple. I left that part out."

"Stand Up," Adam read aloud. "That's your name?"

"Yep. It's based on that quote about falling for anything. Argyle loved it and my presentation."

"What did you say to her?" I asked.

"I told her our purpose was to educate and support causes in the local community. On weekends, we'll volunteer or fundraise. I said our meeting place could be in the multipurpose room since it's shared by both campuses, and since more is better with an organization like this, we can keep it out of the battle system so they don't have to worry about their 'no boys against girls' rule."

"Wow. You thought of everything."

"Totally. I was ready for every single argument she might have." She rolled her eyes. "Ready, but still I couldn't get everything. She wouldn't agree to keep it out of the battle system.

Anyone can come to meetings, but she said standard rules apply to volunteer opportunities, you have to battle for it."

"But this isn't about volunteering," Adam spoke up. "We're protesting the system."

She looked around before leaning in. "Yes, we are and everyone signing up knows it. Today's bullshit only makes me more determined. Where do they get off saying our personal things are up for battle too?"

Melody slid the clipboard across the table. "You guys sign and put your numbers. Official meetings are on Thursdays, but I'll text you when and where the *real* meeting will be."

Adam slid out the pen and signed without hesitation.

Someone gripped me under the table. "Zeke," Owen whispered. "Incoming."

I knew before I looked up who it must be. Cameron strode across the cafeteria, eyes fixed on us. He didn't have his shadow or shadows trailing him, but he didn't need them to cause trouble.

My eyes narrowed. *Let him come. I'm going to find out what game he's playing by forcing Landon to battle me. This ends now.*

I rose to my feet as Cameron stopped before our table. "What do you want, Cameron?"

He smiled—that dazzling smile that made you want to believe no one this beautiful could have a bad bone in his body.

"Just wondering if you're going to eat dinner with me, baby?"

My mind, and the hundreds of comebacks it was prepping, came to a crashing halt.

What did he just call me?!

His eyes flicked down. "I saved you my slice of cheesecake. I know it's your favorite."

"Aww. Thank you." Melody popped out of the chair and faced Cameron.

No. No, no, no.

She threw her arms around him and planted a searing kiss on those grinning lips.

No!

The word tried to escape my throat, but it was too tight to let anything but a strangle squeak out. This was worse. This was so much worse. Why couldn't Cameron have been talking to me?

Reluctantly, I glanced at Adam. The look on his face as he saw them kiss almost broke me. His face drained of color—jaw slack as the pen fell from his fingers.

Melody came up for air. "Thank you, but I have to get these signatures while everyone is here. We can have breakfast together tomorrow."

"Sounds perfect." He flicked her nose, making her giggle.

Cameron turned his smile on us. "I see you're joining too, Moon. You know, I never got a chance to thank you."

Melody looked from him to a silent Adam. "Thank him for what?"

"It's because of him that we're together," he said clearly. "During orientation, he told me about this smart, beautiful, amazing girl named Melody that used to go to our middle school. When I ran into you at the Promenade, I knew I had to get to know you this time." I didn't know if anyone else noticed it, but I saw an edge to his smile. "It's all thanks to you, Moon."

"Oh, Adam." Melody released Cameron and went over to him. "I keep saying you're the sweetest guy ever and it's true. I can't believe we weren't friends in middle school, but I'm glad we're friends now."

Slowly, and with pain I couldn't imagine, Adam smiled. "I am too, Melody."

Adam slid the clipboard to me and got to his feet. "Sorry, but I have to go. I forgot I was meeting up with my mom."

She waved him off. "Bye. I'll text you soon."

He didn't reply or slow his stride. Adam walked calmly out of the dining room while I stood there with no clue what to do.

"Zeke?"

I took my eyes off the doorway he disappeared from and saw Melody was holding out the board and pen. Quickly, I signed and she left with a thank you.

Cameron didn't follow right away. He tossed me one last wink before turning and walking off.

I stared at his retreating back as it finally dawned on me who I was dealing with. He said the Elite needed to find weaknesses and exploit them ruthlessly. But this was ruthless on a level that made me physically sick.

"Zeke?" Owen asked. "Are you okay?"

"No," I said as I sat down. "I'm not."

ORLOV SAID THERE SHOULDN'T be any trouble scheduling our battle and he was right. Thursday dawned bright and clear—more than perfect for the history/soccer battle that was going to take place at two o'clock on the dot.

Dawson walked on my right side while Adam walked on the other. I snuck glances at my friend as we headed up the stairs.

He had been quiet since we found out about Melody and Cameron two days before. I tried to talk to him that night, but he said Melody was free to date whoever she wanted. I went another way and said we had to warn her that Cameron was just using her, but he pointed out that we didn't have proof and she had no reason to believe us over her boyfriend. Then he left the room and I took that as a signal he didn't want to talk about it anymore.

Things had been weird ever since. It didn't help that Melody still popped over to our table at dinner and breakfast to say hi, often with Cameron in tow. Everything in me wanted to tell her that Cam was a snake, but Adam was right. She's only known me for what amounted to less than two weeks. Why would she believe me?

"Are you ready, Zeke?"

I pulled myself out of my thoughts and looked over at my teacher. "Honestly, no. I've had history class with you for less than a week, and you weren't allowed to tell me what would be on the test."

"I told you what I could," he said. "The test will be limited to information expressly in your textbook. No tricks. Mr. Orlov and I will proctor the test and then we'll go straight to the field for the match. Afterward, we'll calculate the scores and you'll find out if you won by tomorrow."

"Okay," I said, although none of that reassured me. I studied as much as I could over the last few days, and my gym clothes were on and fresh. I was as ready for this as I would ever be.

"Adam, if you want to come, you'll have to wait outside."

Together, the three of us stepped up to the Elite floor landing. I led the way to Orlov's class and threw open the door. I froze when I noticed there were more than two people inside.

Orlov, Landon, Michael, Cole, Zach, and Derek looked up from their desks.

"Ah. Right on time, Mr. Manning," Orlov said. He had the nerve to smile at me. "You will be at Mr. Reed's desk. Gentlemen, step out so we can begin the battle."

One by one, they stood up and filed out of the room. Derek was the last to leave. He brushed past me, close enough he bumped my shoulder. "We need to talk after this," he whispered.

"What?" I turned around just as the door closed in my face.

"Sit down, Mr. Manning. Let's get started."

Taking a steadying breath, I headed to Cole's desk and took a seat, chancing a look at Landon on the way. He didn't meet my eyes.

"Okay, now we'll begin," Orlov announced. "The test is simple. You'll have thirty minutes to write two to three paragraphs answering a question about an event in U.S. history." He came around and placed a pencil and a single sheet of paper facedown on our desks. "When I call time, you will put your pencil down. If you do not, you will receive an automatic fail on the academic test. Understood?"

"Yes, sir."

"Yes, Mr. Orlov."

"Then..." He lifted his phone and tapped the screen. "Begin."

We flipped our papers over at the same time.

"Describe one way the New Deal helped each of the following groups: the unemployed, farmers, and the factory workers."

I stared at the words. My hand made no move to take the pencil. To my right, I heard faint scratching as Landon began to write.

No. Oh no. This can't be happening.

I couldn't answer the question. I didn't have a flipping clue what the New Deal was, let alone how this mysterious thing helped these groups of people.

I lifted my head...

...and looked into Orlov's eyes. He was fixed on me and he was still smiling.

I dropped my gaze, but staring at the paper wasn't much better. I don't know how long I sat there, wracking my brain for information that would never come, before I finally picked up my pencil and wrote something for the mere sake of not wanting to hand in a blank piece of paper.

"Time's up."

I dropped my pencil without a problem.

"Let's go, boys. Off to the field."

Standing on legs that shook, I half stumbled as I trailed Landon to the door. I had failed. There was no question about it. I had failed for the first time in my life. Not that Mom didn't teach me with a grading system, but she always worked with me until I understood whatever lesson she was teaching me, so there was never a day that I walked away from the table as a failure.

Until now.

"Are you alright, Mr. Manning?" Orlov asked as he held open the door. "You look quite pale."

"I'm fine."

I walked out and found Adam where I expected him to be, but he wasn't alone. Derek stood by his side while Cole, Michael, and Zach posted up on the other wall.

Without a word, the five of them fell in step behind us as we moved to the soccer field. I didn't bother to ask why they were coming.

Coach Fineman was a lone figure by the bleachers as we approached. "Foster. Manning. Stand in front of me."

We glanced at each other before doing as he said. Coach cast his eyes over us like he was sizing us up. "The rules are this. One-on-one match that will last no more than thirty minutes. There are no goalies of course, so this is all about speed, quick thinking, and having the skill to hang on to the ball. Whoever has the most points at the end wins."

The rules sounded simple, but I knew it would be anything but. That was okay. I had chosen soccer because Landon was just as bad at it as I was.

This is my chance to make up some points, I thought as I jogged onto the field.

Fifteen minutes into the game, I knew I was screwed. The Landon who tripped over balls and ran into people during orientation was nowhere to be found. The boy raced up and down the grass, kicking and knocking the ball about like an old pro while I wheezed after him. I attempted my soccer math every time I managed to get it away from him, but he'd be right on me, so close I felt his breath on my neck.

I made two shots. Landon made one, two, three, four, five—

Fweeeet!

"Time's up!" Fineman bellowed as his fifth shot sailed into the welcoming arms of the net. "Players, get some water."

I trudged off the field, head hanging. I lost. I lost my first trial. I lost the chair. I lost to Cameron.

Derek and Adam stood up.

"It's okay," said Adam. "You might still win."

"It's not okay," I rasped. "I don't need to wait until tomorrow to find out the score. I can give him the chair right now. I didn't know the answer to the history question, and you saw what happened out there. I thought Landon wasn't good at soccer."

Derek scoffed. "Maybe he wasn't at orientation, but the guy lives in a house as big as this school. He must have hired someone to teach him over the summer for this very reason. He can't have anyone thinking he has a weakness in battle."

That was the final wind out of my sail. My shoulders slumped. "Of course, he did. I never stood a chance. If Cameron was looking to see me humiliated, it worked."

"No, Zeke. That's not what this is about."

I blinked. Something in Adam's voice forced me to straighten. He wasn't looking at me. Following his gaze, I spotted Landon, Cole, Michael, and Zach standing on the other side of the bleachers—watching us.

"What is it about, then?" I asked.

"Landon was put up to it by Cameron," Derek began. "He said Landon should consider himself on probation and if he doesn't do what he says, he's out of the Network. There's a reason they chose U.S. history. You don't know much about the States."

"Yes, I d—"

"No, Zeke," he cut in. "You don't. You proved it during orientation when you didn't have a clue about what happened at Evergreen Academy or to Michael's mom. Both those stories were national news for weeks and you never heard about it.

"Cameron got it into his head that maybe you didn't know about what went on in the U.S. at all. For someone who has traveled to twenty-six countries, how likely is it that your mom would spend all her time teaching you about one?"

"Mom did teach me about the Revolution and the Civil War and stuff. She just— She wanted me to know about the places we lived in—"

Derek looked at me steadily as I tripped over my response. It felt like a betrayal to say that he was right. My mom had taught me well and I loved that I was raised on world history, but—

"No," I forced out. "I don't know much, but that's why I'm here. I'm taking history."

"You are, but until you catch up, this will be your weakness in battle. Cameron wants it exploited until you've got nothing else. It's not going to stop at your chair."

I gaped at him. "How do you know this? Did you overhear him?"

"I didn't have to. He wasn't hiding it. Cameron strolled into our class today and told Landon all of this with me sitting right behind him. He doesn't care if I know *or* if you do."

I worked to get a handle on what he was telling me. "Doesn't care if I know? What does that mean?"

Neither Derek nor Adam had an answer for me.

Taking a deep breath, I held it and then let it out slowly. "I'm tired. I'm going back to my dorm, cleaning up, and then I'll work on figuring out what's up."

"*We* will figure it out," Adam corrected. He shook his head, making his curls fly. "Whatever that son of a bitch is trying to pull, we're going to put a stop to it. Right, Derek?"

The other boy shrugged.

"Not overly eager, Grayson, but I'll take any help I can get."

"I barely know your ass," he replied, but there was a small smile playing on his lips.

"Seriously, guys. Thanks."

Adam clapped my shoulder. "Of course, Zeke. Now let's get out of here. They're creeping me out."

They definitely were. The Elites stared at us as we walked past them. We made it three steps before someone spoke up.

"Manning."

"Yes, Cole?"

"There's something I need to tell you."

I paused and turned to face him. "What is it?"

Cole closed the distance between us until his sweet, citrusy smell invaded my lungs. Even scowling he was heartbreakingly handsome.

"Manning," he said softly. "I challenge you to a battle in history."

Michael stepped up next to him. "Zeke, I challenge you to a battle in history."

Landon took his other side. "I challenge you to a battle in history."

My head snapped between them. "Wait, guys. You don't—"

"Manning." Zach pushed through them. There was a grin on his face that turned my stomach. "I challenge you to a battle in history. Let's go find Orlov. I'm sure he'll be happy to approve us."

Chapter Four

"Has it really been that bad?"

I gave Jordan a look as I opened the trunk. "It's been worse than bad." I peeked around the hood to make sure our moms were still inside. "They've taken everything that Mom bought me. My chair, my mattress pad, my trunk, my rug, my sheets, my pillows—"

"What?!" she cried. "They've taken your sheets and pillows? What do you sleep with?"

School started a month ago and it had been awful with constant battles. The moment I finished one, there was another one coming up to challenge me—always in history. I was driving myself nuts reading ahead in the history textbook and making Adam, Tanner, and Nico test me every chance we got. It still wasn't enough.

"The housekeepers had to get me spares from the laundry. I'm back to the brownish-white sheets and limp pillows like the rest of my dorm."

Jordan made a face. "Ick. I can't believe this, Zee. You have to do something. Challenge them too."

I shook my head. "It's not that simple."

"How is it not that simple? The whole point of the school is to battle, so battle those bitches! Get your stuff back!"

"Those bitches are smart, Jo. They're in the Elite Class because they don't have weak subjects."

She threw out her hands. "So?! You're smart too."

"Yes, but I'm in the F Class, and the rules say the academic test can't be on anything that isn't in the lowest student's curriculum."

She was still staring blankly at me.

"My curriculum is super basic!" I burst out. "English I, Algebra I, Biology. They can ace that stuff in their sleep. Even if I battle them in algebra, we'd most likely both get hundreds, then they beat me on the physical test and I still lose."

"Oh," she breathed. "And of course, they all kill at sports."

"You know they do. They run faster than me. Swimming is off the table. They're twice my size so wrestling is out. That leaves basketball and soccer but the calculating still slows me down which is death in a one-on-one match."

"But why can't you do the academic tests on your level? There's no way they're as good at math as you. Give you a calculus test and you'll have them all crying under their desks."

"They won't do that because I'm in the *F* Class. I'm fucked, Jordan. That's what the F stands for!" I snatched up a grocery bag and slammed the trunk harder than necessary.

"Damn," I heard her say as I stormed off. "You hate saying the f-word, my saintly cousin. You must be pissed."

"I am. Turns out I hate losing as much as I hate flunking. Mom was a great teacher. Everyone used to say how gifted I was, but now when Orlov walks up to me, smiling as he puts that stupid history test down, I feel like an idiot. Why don't I know this?"

Jordan caught me on the steps of the porch and swung me around. "Hey. Don't talk about yourself like that. No one can learn hundreds of years of history in one month. You can't even learn it in a semester which is why teachers skip to the important crap." She planted her hands on her hips. "And if you ask me, this Orlov guy sounds like he's enjoying this too much. What was the question on the last test he gave you?"

I rattled it off without hesitation. My latest failure and the loss of my mattress pad was burned in my brain. "Why do historians use the word revolution to describe changes in the industry and in transportation from the time period 1790 to 1860?"

She snapped her fingers. "See."

"See what?"

"That's super hard. How were you supposed to remember that?"

"It was in the textbook. I looked up all the answers afterward. He didn't trick me."

"No, what he did was blow past all the major, important events in U.S. history that he knew you would be cramming for, and go with the random factoids that no one remembers. Why did they call it a revolution? Who the hell cares? *I* don't even know that and I've had more U.S. history classes than you."

I let out a breath. "I guess it's possible. If he does have his choice of questions, he could be picking the more obscure ones. But like I said, I looked them up and it's straight out of my textbook. I don't have anything to go to Argyle with. I can't do anything, Jordan."

"That's not true." Jordan stomped up the stairs, advancing on me fast. My eyes went round when I suddenly had her in my face. "You can fight back and I don't care what level you're at."

Jordan's eyes were blazing. I've never seen her this worked up. "If you need to learn history, then read every history textbook in that school. I'll even help you study. If you need to get better at sports, then woman up and get someone to teach you like those rich boys did. You turn the tables on them and you start taking *their* shit! And you tell this Cameron bitch that if he keeps messing with you, I'm coming for him! Got it?"

Stunned, I nodded fast. "Got it."

She sniffed. "Good. Now, let's go inside. The milk is getting warm."

After a minute, I followed her into her house, my mind whirling.

Jordan had given me an idea.

THAT NIGHT, I SPENT longer than needed combing out my hair. I was enjoying letting it fall around my shoulders instead of pinned and suffocated under a wig. I was Zela again and I loved it. I had been coming home every weekend since school started and it was no mystery why.

Zela slept in a cozy bedroom. Zela wore what she liked. Zela didn't have to take a test or run across a field to eat a slice of pizza.

Knock. Knock.

I heard the creak of my bedroom door opening. "Zela?"

"In the bathroom, Mom. I'll be out in a minute."

I set down my comb and pulled my hair into a messy bun. Mom was sitting on my bed when I came out.

"I thought we should talk before I drive you back to school tomorrow."

"Is this about my undercover work?" I bounced on the bed, inhaling the sweet scent of detergent from my freshly washed sheets. "I've talked to Melody, and the new rules have been worse for the girls' side. The upper classes have been taking advantage and going after the F girls because one of the Elites ran her mouth at the beginning of the year and said the Fs should have just been kicked out. It caused a fight and now they're basically at war. Melody has tried to cool things down and remind them that they should be mad at the system, not each other."

"But it is not her responsibility to cool things down," said Mom. "How has the administration handled this?"

"Melody says Argyle and Whittaker are happy to see the number of challenges to the F students going up. They think it's good for them."

"Hera, help us." Sighing, Mom leaned back onto my pillows. "And what do you think about this?"

"I think..." I took a minute to chew over my thoughts. "I've been thinking of what you told me about revolutions. The number of peaceful revolutions that have brought about change are outnumbered by violent ones because people don't give up power easily. In human history, it has to be taken. Right now, the Elite have all the power and they won't give it up even if it hurts the rest of us." My silk sheets rumpled in my fist. "Soon people will get tired of it and they'll fight back."

A hand rested gently on top of my head. "That is very likely, my Zela. If fights are breaking out, the unease is starting to boil over." She stroked my hair the way she used to do when I was little. "Has it begun to affect you? You left your student handbook on the counter last week. I know the depth of the class separation and it's nothing you've ever dealt with before."

I turned my head slightly away, letting the curtain of my hair block my eyes. "I've been through much worse, Mom."

Her hand stilled. "Yes... you have. But that situation was out of your control, this one is not. Have you been hearing the voices again?"

I shook my head, making her hand fall off. "I haven't heard voices for a long time," I lied.

"I just want to be sure a war is not brewing on your side of campus as well. I won't have a harmless experiment become a cause of stress and trauma. Have the male Elites been targeting the F students as well?"

"They aren't going after the F students."

Just one.

"That is something at least. Are you certain you still wish to attend?"

"I do."

"All right." She patted my head once more. "Then run down, get the pea crisps, and we can finish watching that movie from last week. You were right about the Japanese filmmaker. He does an admirable job crafting strong female characters. It's prompted me to add a section in the book about female empowerment through film."

"That's cool, Mom. I just really like the part where No-Face goes on a rampage and tries to eat everyone."

She heaved a sigh. "Oh, Zela."

Laughing, I raced out to get the snacks while she queued up the movie.

I WAVED GOODBYE TO Mom and Jordan through the windshield. So started another week at Breakbattle.

Adam looked up from his laptop when I came into the dorm.

"Hello, roomie," I announced. "How was your weekend?"

He shrugged. "I helped Mom and Jaxson fix up the nursery, and Ryder took me into the office on Saturday. You?"

"My weekend was amazing. I slept at my cousin's house Friday night and then spent all day Saturday watching movies and plotting."

"I'm sorry. Did you just say plotting?"

"Jordan gave me an idea for how to put a stop to"—I gestured at my bare side of the room—"this."

"How?"

"Step one: I need Derek."

Adam groaned. "This plan is doomed."

"Hey. He hasn't been so bad. Derek's nice now."

"Compared to orientation, you can use the word nice, but when stacking Derek Grayson against normal humans? He made a kid cry last week for asking if he could get his mother's autograph."

Huffing, I crossed the room and tossed my backpack on the bed. "That guy came running up to our table out of nowhere when we were in the middle of talking. He couldn't even be bothered with a please. Derek's tongue is a little... sharp, but that guy was rude."

"You do that a lot."

"Do what?"

"Defend him."

I gave him my back as I put away the things I brought from home. "Because he's my friend."

"Does he feel the same way?"

"I guess I'll find out." I faced him as I turned to sit down. "Do you remember his room number?"

"Top floor. Room 612."

"Great. I'll be right back."

"Can't wait to hear how this goes," he called as I slipped out of the room.

I shook my head. Adam and Derek's relationship had been shaky since the animal crackers, but it was different with us. Derek didn't tolerate people he didn't like. Him paying any attention to me at all was tantamount to a love confession.

I climbed the stairs to the sixth floor and paused before the entrance. There was a tiny window in the door that let me see inside. A couple of boys were milling around in the hall, chatting to each other from their doorways.

I hesitated. There was no way I was making it through them without a comment.

What does that matter? You're not afraid of them, Zela. They don't own this school.

My mental pep talk pushed me forward. I opened the door and strode in, head high. I made it as far as room 608 before Heath caught sight of me.

"What's this? What are you doing here?"

"None of your business, Dowell."

"What did you say?" Heath shoved out of the doorway. "Watch yourself, F."

A rude noise drew my attention to the boy across from Heath. Santiago stepped out of the room, staring me down with no trace of his patented bored expression. "I can't believe we ever thought this guy was Elite material. Failed every single battle he's been in. Pathetic."

His jab struck me like a hot poker, burning me inside. "I can't be that pathetic," I blurted. "Or Mrs. Peterson wouldn't have gushed about me being the most promising math student she's ever seen. A prodigy."

His eyes flashed. "You're lying. She never said that!"

I grinned. "You're right. She didn't." I lifted my hand and rapped on 612. "But you should have seen your face. If you didn't think I was Elite material, why are you so threatened by me?"

"Me? Threatened? You're not on my level, Homeschooler."

"And you don't belong here," Heath added. "Get off our floor."

I raised my chin and looked him in the eyes. "No."

Heath and Santiago moved at the same time. They stomped down the hall, advancing on me quick.

"We said to leave!"

Derek's door swung open. "Manning? What the hell are you doing—"

Moving fast, I ducked under his arm and shot inside just as Santiago's hand closed over the spot my head had been.

"What the— What do you two want?!"

"Move, Grayson," Heath demanded. "He doesn't belong here. We're going to escort the F back to his place."

"You're not coming in my room."

Santi moved in front of Heath. His bulk filled the doorway, casting a shadow on both of us. "Don't start your bullshit. We know you pretend to be his friend to piss off Cam, but you're a brother now. You're one of us. Move aside."

"Damn. If we're brothers, why don't I remember your oversized ass at the end of my dining table growing up? The F leaves when I say so." He reeled back and slammed the door so fast Santiago didn't have time to blink. He swiftly locked it before the banging started.

I gazed at the back of his head, chest heaving. I didn't like him fighting my battles for me, but Santiago was twice my size and backed up by a guy who clearly worked out as much as he did. If they got hold of me, I wasn't getting free.

"It's not true."

"What?" I said. "What isn't?"

Derek turned to face me. "I don't hang out with you to piss him off."

"I know."

"That would mean I gave a shit about what Cameron thinks or feels."

"And you don't give a shit what anyone thinks or feels."

The corner of his mouth quirked up in the tiniest smile. "You're learning, Manning." He pushed off the door and brushed past me. "So what do you want?"

I turned as he flung himself on the bed. Free in his room, his uniform was nowhere to be found. Derek was comfortable in a pair of loose sweats that hung low on his hips and a sleeveless tank. His casual vibe was at complete odds with this fancy space.

I thought I knew what the Elite rooms would look like after being in the A dorm, but I had no idea. The bed was bigger. The desk was bigger. The television was bigger. He had two wardrobes instead of one and I was pretty sure the expensive desktop computer I was looking at came with the room. The entire budget that could have made the F dorms look less like an abandoned building in a horror movie had clearly been funneled here.

It wasn't fair to be sure, but it wasn't jealousy that was twinging as I looked around the space. It was curiosity. It wasn't much, but scattered over the room were little insights into Derek. The basketball propped up in the corner next to his gym bag. The stack of books on his bedside table. The complete lack of family or friend photos.

"Manning?"

I stopped gawking and reached for Derek's desk chair. I wheeled it over to his bed. "I'm here because I want your help."

"My help?"

"Yes," I said as I sat down. "I was sleeping over at my cousin's house—"

"You still have sleepovers? How old are you?" He lifted a brow. "What do you two do all night?"

"We talk about gross assholes who insinuate there's something wrong with being close with your cousin."

He barked a laugh.

"Anyway," I continued. "While we were talking about assholes, we got onto this whole thing with the Elites stripping me of everything I've got and she told me I should do what you guys do. I need to get someone to teach me so I can do better on the physical tests. I need you."

His brows shot up his forehead. "Me? What do you expect me to do?"

"I want you to teach me so I can get better at basketball."

"Isn't that Coach Singh's job?"

"He's got thirty-six other students and he's teaching every single one of them as slow as he's teaching me. We're still working on the right way to dribble." I leaned in, placing my hands on the bed. "I'll learn so much faster if I do it one-on-one with you."

He clicked his tongue. "Trying to use me to replace Mommy? I don't have time to homeschool."

I didn't let his harsh tone faze me. By now I knew his default mode was jerk. I just needed to keep pushing till I found the decent guy buried deep. "If you're really sorry about what you did to me at orientation, then you'll make time."

Derek frowned. "You think throwing that in my face is your best move? I didn't have a choice, Manning."

"But I did." I held his gaze without flinching. "I had a choice and I chose to do the right thing for you because you're my friend."

His frown was deepening and I can't say that response was reassuring, but I kept on.

"All I'm asking is for a few pointers because I'm not putting up with this anymore. I'm going to challenge them. I'm going to win the physical tests, and I'm going to get my stuff back. You can help me." I leaned in closer. "You *will* help me because you're my friend whether you admit it or not."

Derek said nothing. He stared at me for so long, my back began to ache from being hunched over the bed. Still, I didn't move.

"You believe that's going to work?" he finally said. "Even their worst basketballer, Cole, is light years better than you. You're too slow."

"If anyone can help me improve my game, it's you. You're that good."

He inclined his head. "That is true, but still…"

I held my breath. It had to be him. Adam hated basketball. Tanner and Nico weren't good at it. The only other guy I knew who was on Derek's level was Cameron Dupre, and he was not an option.

"All right."

"Really?" I jumped up. "You mean it?"

"Yep. I practice after detention to keep sharp for when try-outs open up again. You can join me and I'll give some tips."

Squealing, I bounced on my heels. "Thank you. Thank you."

"But you weren't my friend."

I stopped bouncing. "What?"

"During orientation," he went on. "You said you had my back because you were my friend, but I wasn't yours. Couldn't stand you."

"I remember."

"Thought you were a stalker."

"I know," I said quickly. "We don't need to talk about it."

Derek's eyes were unfocused as he recalled my torment. "An obsessed fanboy with a pic of me in your pants."

"In my pants?!" I snatched up a pillow and flung it at his head. "May I remind you all I did was try to talk to you in the cafeteria?"

The pillow caught him full in the face and he fell over laughing. "Yeah. You did and I treated you like shit. Which is why I'm shocked you were the one who refused to go with Cameron." He propped himself up, a grin on his face. "You're actually a good guy while Cameron Dupre is a walking trash bag. If helping you win battles will stop whatever he's trying to pull, then I'll do it."

"Oh," I said softly. Warmth began in my toes and spread through my body, filling me up as that smile graced me. "Thanks." I smiled back. "I knew you were my friend."

"I never said that. Don't get carried away."

But he was still smiling.

I looked away as the urge to squeal came roaring back. *This is going so well. He's going to help me. I know he wouldn't do that for just anyone. He likes me. I know he does.*

Eyes pointed away, I caught something as Derek straightened up.

"How'd you get that?" I asked, pointing to the faint scar on his foot.

"This? I was running in the figurine room and knocked a table over. They broke and a piece of flying glass sliced my foot open."

"It matches mine." I bent over and took the shoe and sock off my right foot. I propped it on the chair so he could see. "Got it from a machete."

"What?" He actually leaned in closer for a better look at the faint scar below my pinky toe. "You did not."

"It's true. We lived in a village where everyone had one. You used it for food and defense, but I dropped ours on my foot like a genius. To be fair, I was nine."

He laughed. "Check this out." Derek lifted his forearm. "Got this burn when I was four. The housekeeper said I couldn't touch the cookie tray, but I went for it anyway. Turned out it just came from the oven."

"I got this abseiling." I climbed on the bed and twisted around to show off the scar at the nape of my neck. "They say not to close your eyes. I didn't listen."

"Abseiling?" he said between chuckles. "You? I can't see you jumping off any cliffs."

"Why not? I'm tough."

Derek laughed even harder. "Let's see these machete-wielding, abseiling pics."

"I've got pictures!" I scrambled for my phone. "You should have seen me walking across the cloud bridge. I—" I halted as common sense returned. I couldn't show him pictures. *Zela* was in those pictures, not Zeke.

I shoved the phone back in my pocket. "Actually, I forgot to transfer them."

"Suuurrreee," he drew out.

"You're just going to have to trust me. I trust you." I grinned. "I have no trouble believing you've gotten burned and banged up from being a brat."

"Oh ho," he cried. "Zeke came to play. I'm going to give you that one though because that's for sure how it went down. I've also got a scar on my back from when Dad got me the wrong colt and I yelled at him to give it back. It kicked me because it knew."

I laughed so hard I almost fell off the bed. "Oh my goodness. What did your dad do?"

"He sold it, of course. I just said the vindictive animal kicked me."

We busted up.

This couldn't have been more perfect if I planned it. Derek and I finally alone, bonding. Not to mention the time I would spend with him improving my game.

"Hold on a sec." Derek got off the bed and went to the door. He stuck his head out. "Yep. Santi and Heath are still there," he said as he came back in. "You think they want to wave you goodbye on your way out?"

"I do not think that."

He laughed. "You better stick around until they give up."

I bit down hard on my smile. It wouldn't do to give myself away. "Okay. That's cool with me."

THREE HOURS LATER, I slipped out into an empty hallway. The Elites had finally given up.

The stairwell was quiet except for the squeaks of my sneakers.

Hope Adam is still in the room so I can catch him up before dinner. We—

I pulled open the door and froze. Cameron smirked as he peeled himself off the wall.

"You had to come down sometime."

"So you've been standing here waiting for me? That's not creepy at all."

Cameron laughed—a soft, husky sound that drew a shiver up my spine. Why was he here? And what did it mean that he was alone?

"I heard from Heath and Santi that you've been running your mouth. You're real confident for someone who has racked up eight battle losses."

I raised my chin. "I'm confident for someone who isn't going to lose anymore. I don't know what you were trying to accomplish by getting them to take my stuff, but I'm going to get it all back."

Cameron cocked his head. "You don't know? Really? But I thought it was so obvious." He took a step, then another, until he was inches from me. "The Elite Network welcomed you. We wanted you to be one of us but you spat in our faces. You refused to trust your brothers and I'm making you pay for it by exploiting your weakness."

He bent down until our noses almost brushed. "You've always been the smart one. No one to tell you differently because there were no kids to compare yourself to. You got to be Mommy's little genius, but here you're average— No, you're less than average. At least most of the dumbasses here know their history. You don't know anything.

"You're stupid, Zeke," he whispered. "You're stupid and you're slow and you're not good enough to be in a regular school. Your little tricks with math might have been impressive in some jungle village no one cares about, but here, it's not enough."

He stepped around me, pressing against my back as he put his mouth to my ear. "And every time you lose, you'll be forced to accept it. You'll trudge back to this shit heap, go into your empty room, and know you couldn't defend yourself or your stuff because you're an F. F is where you belong. F is what you are. So run your mouth all you want. We both know you'll never be able to back it up. I'm waiting for you to admit defeat. When you do, I'm willing to talk terms."

Cam's presence faded as I heard the door open and softly close shut. My whole body was trembling. Fury coursed through my veins, white hot and corrosive. I had never felt an emotion like this. One that made me want to punch him in his perfect smile, tear out his hair, and fling back every dagger he threw at me.

With a few words, Cam had stripped me and laid my insecurities bare. It made me wish Santiago and Heath had been waiting for me instead.

"THERE YOU ARE," ADAM said when I came in. "How'd it go with Derek?"

I slammed the door, making him jump. "Great. He's going to help me with my basketball so I can get back my stuff and show Cameron who he is messing with!"

Adam blinked. "Um. Are you okay?"

"I'm going to show him who's stupid!" I cried. I stomped over to my bed and threw myself down. "He thinks he's getting to me but it's not going to work. I will *not* lose another battle!"

"I'm glad to hear it, man. Don't let him win."

I nodded sharply. "You're not going to let him win either, Adam. You don't want to tell Melody about the real him, then you don't have to. You just have to let her see the real you. She likes you."

He pinked. "She doesn't—"

"She does. She thinks you're cute and sweet and charming. Everything that Cameron is pretending to be. If you spend more time with her, she'll see you're the real deal and dump Cameron all on her own."

"Zeke, it's not that—"

I jumped up and towered over him. "Do you want to be with Melody or not?"

He stared at me, wide eyes, until his expression changed. I watched as steel set his jaw. "I do."

"Then show her you're the one who really cares about her."

He nodded. "You know, I've never seen you like this before."

"I've never been this pissed off before," I replied, but the truth was I was calming down. The red mist was clearing as my resolve took root. I was going to learn every single bit of U.S. history. I would become so good at sports; I'd earn the title prodigy for real. I would show him who belonged at Breakbattle. "This is my school. I came here for a reason and I'm sick of Cameron getting in the way."

"I'm sick of Cameron period. I thought it'd be fun to go to school with my friends, but instead we're all split up and Zach's gone over to the dark side. No more. I'm going to enjoy high school no matter what's going on." He pointed at me. "You should come over my house this weekend."

"What?"

"Come on. All we've done is study and obsess about Cameron. Mom said that you could stay over, so let's do it. We'll hang out and have fun. What do you think?"

"Okay. I have to ask my mom first, but I'd like that."

He grinned. "Nice. But since it's not the weekend yet. Tell me about this plan to turn things around on Cameron."

I help up a finger. "First, Derek. Then..."

Adam and I stayed up late into the night, going over our plans. Cameron's words rang in my ears the whole time.

I would prove him wrong. It was now my second mission in life.

Chapter Five

"Look. There she is."

"Don't point!"

I quickly dropped my hand, fighting a laugh.

Slowly, Adam peered over his shoulder. Melody glided across the room with her clique on her heels. If she started the year in their bad books for being Elite, they had forgiven her now.

Adam rose as she picked up her tray. I watched as he went over to her, said something, and walked next to her as she got her food. The two left the line and came over to our table together.

"Hi, Zeke," she said as she pulled out the chair next to me. "How was your weekend?"

"It was good. I got my mom hooked on anime."

Smiling, she rolled her eyes. "You boys and your anime. They're just a bunch of cartoons."

Yep. Us boys.

I stifled a giggle at my private joke. "Because we're friends, I'll let the cartoon thing slide."

She laughed. "Anyway, I was just telling Adam about next Friday."

Melody looked from side to side. This was her tell that club business was about to be spilled. She leaned across Adam, brushing up against his arm.

"We're having our first protest at the basketball game."

"The basketball game?"

She nodded. "We'll make the posters this week during the club meeting. During the game, we'll come in, take our seats, and hold up our End The Battle System posters."

"Argyle will flip," I said.

"She will, but we have a right to protest whether she likes it or not. Ours will be silent. We're not going to scream, throw paint, or go where we're not allowed, so she can't say we're being disruptive." She looked between us. "What do you guys think? Are you in?"

"I'm in," said Adam before I could open my mouth. "All this stuff with Zeke is just proof the system needs to be done away with. This school can have advanced classes like the rest of them do and leave it at that. They don't need to go out of their way to make people feel different."

Melody clapped the table. "Exactly. See, Adam, you get it. It's a step too far and it's bringing out the worst in people."

"I'm in too," I spoke up.

She beamed. "Thanks, guys." Melody squeezed Adam's arm. "I knew I could count on you. I'm going to sit with my friends, but I'll see you at the meeting."

I waved her off, waiting until she was out of earshot to speak. "Wow. She *really* does like you."

"Wha— No! What?" His curls were bouncing as he roughly shook his head. "You can't know that."

"Of course I can." I reached for my cup of peaches and speared a bite. "She touched your arm."

"So?"

I gave him a knowing look. "She's always touching you, brushing against your arm, squeezing your shoulder—all of it. She doesn't touch me that much."

A rosy-pink hue was staining his cheeks. No wonder Melody liked him. The guy was adorable.

"That doesn't mean she likes me."

"Yes, it does," I said around a mouthful of peaches. "Trust me. I know women."

"Oh yeah? How?"

I stopped chewing. *Damn. My mouth gets Zeke into so much trouble.*

"Because I was raised by one," I finally said.

"I was too, but I'm clueless."

"Yes. Yes, you are."

Laughing, he shoved my shoulder and I fell against the table giggling.

I was feeling pretty good about Adam's side of things. Even if they never got together, if they got close enough that she would believe his word against Cameron, that was good enough. He was a nasty guy and she deserved better.

It was my side of things that were tough.

After classes let out that day, I waited a few feet from the bottom of the stairs as the upper floors emptied out. There was one boy in particular I needed.

I spotted Landon immediately. Only his head was visible in the sea of identically clad boys, but I knew it was him. I waited for him to get closer before I called.

"Landon?"

He stopped and sought me over the noise. When he faced me, I saw his eyes were gold today. "Something I can do for you, Manning?"

"I love that you put it that way because yes, there is something you can do." I stepped closer and lowered my voice. "I need to talk to you in private. Come to the basketball court at three."

I walked off before he could get a word out. I was leaning on curiosity to make him come.

Derek had detention, so I took my things to the court to wait. Landon found me an hour later sitting on the bleachers doing homework.

"I'm here, Manning." His leather shoes squeaked on the polished maple floors as he closed the distance between us. "What do you want?"

Unhurriedly, I closed my history textbook and rested my notes on top. Only then did I look up at him. "Landon, did you mean it when you said you weren't on Cameron's side?"

His brows knit together. "Yes. Why?"

"Because if you're really sorry about this, I know a way you can help me." I met his golden eyes. "You can help me win."

"I can what now?"

"You know how to wrestle and play soccer. Teach me."

Pulling a face, Landon looked around like he was waiting for the camera crew to jump out. "What the hell are you talking about, dude? I'm not a coach."

"Just hear me out." I clambered off the bench and ended up eye level with his chest. I breathed deep.

Wow. He always smells so good.

Focus, Zela, scolded my internal voice.

I cleared my throat. "Swimming is off the table and you all run much faster than me. I won't even mention Michael. If I can get better at soccer, wrestling, and basketball, I can turn things around and get my stuff back."

He was still giving me a crazy look. "So you want me... to help you beat me?"

"It sounds weird when you say it like that."

"Is there another way to say it?"

"Yes. I want you to help me beat Cameron."

His expression changed, dropping the this-guy-is-nuts look. "I'm listening."

"He's making you all do this to get back at me. I turned my back on the Network and he wants to make me feel lower than dirt about it. If I start winning, then his stupid plan goes wrong and he may let up on you guys. Let you go back to enjoying your Elite existence instead of battling me for things you don't want."

Landon inclined his head. "I wouldn't mind that. I'm spending all my fucking time studying for history tests when I need to focus on getting on the wrestling team. I want it to stop but it doesn't look good for me to start losing to an F."

"It won't just be you. All of you are going to lose to me."

"You're not doing a great job of selling this," he said, although I glimpsed a grin.

"All I want is my stuff back, Landon. I'm not going to come for your privileges. You really care about losing my pillow?"

He didn't reply, but something stirred behind his eyes. He was considering it.

"You help me and we have a chance to piss off Cameron and end this stupid battle war once and for all. That's a win-win."

"Except for the part where I lose even more of my time teaching you."

I lifted my shoulders. "Think of it as practice. You help me get better and I'll help you."

He hummed. Before I could blink, he reached out and put his arm around me, pulling me to his side. "You know, I always liked you, Homeschooler."

My cheek was burning so hot as it fell against his chest that I was sure he could feel the heat.

"You're a weird guy," he continued. "But interesting. And there aren't many interesting people around here. I'll help you."

I jerked my head up. "You will? Thanks, Land—"

"But not for free," he continued. "Consider yourself my practice dummy 'cause that spot on the team will be mine."

"Oh. Uh." This suddenly seemed like a bad idea. "Okay."

He patted my shoulder. "The soccer field is only free at night so we'll meet after dinner. For wrestling, come by the gym at five. See you."

Just like that, his arm was gone and he was striding away. Landon disappeared through the door moments before Derek walked in.

He was decked out in full gear and his basketball was under his arm.

"Manning, let's do this. There's going to be a battle here in an hour. We don't have a lot of time before we're kicked out."

"Okay. I'm ready."

I jogged over to him and he tossed me the ball. Day one practicing with Derek had begun.

I don't know what I was expecting. Maybe that he would be a taskmaster, but as the practice went on, that guy never showed up. He was surprisingly patient with me.

"I said you can shoot, Manning, but you're so slow." Derek relieved me of the ball and I took the opportunity to wipe the sweat from my brow. Between the wig, bindings, and layers I always felt hot. "What are you thinking about?"

The two of us were standing before the hoop. It had actually been a good practice and I felt I was getting better, but my need to stop and calculate the arc to make it into the hoop had Derek stealing the ball from me every time.

"I'm doing the math," I said.

He frowned. "You said that last time. What is that supposed to mean?"

"I have to calculate the distance, height, and angle of the shot. It's basketball math. It's how it works."

"Basketball math?" I got my second crazy look of the day. "Making a shot isn't about math."

"Yes, it is," I insisted. "It's what you do too, but you don't think about it. Math is in everything and once you figure it out, it all comes together. I just need to calculate faster or"—I glanced around—"if I mentally mark the spots where I need to stand, all I'll have to remember is the angle." I snapped my fingers. "That's it!"

I backed up. "Okay. This is six feet from the hoop. My angle in this spot needs to be—"

"Shut up, dumbass," Derek said with a laugh. "You can't prearrange where you'll be. In a game, everything is going too fast, guys are on your heels, and you'll run up to your spot only to find a dude twice your size ready to 'accidentally' foul you.

"There's no predicting. There's no calculating. Basketball isn't math. It's life." He threw out his hands. "You practice the best you can and then you get out here, everything goes to shit, and from there, instinct takes over. You trust that you know what you're doing and that your team has your back."

I studied his face. There was no trace of meanness or sarcasm. This was a new look on Derek Grayson: passion.

"But I don't know what I'm doing," I finally said. "This is the only way it makes sense to me. Otherwise, I'm just throwing a ball at a circle and hoping for the best."

He laughed. "I'm not saying there's no skill or strategy involved, but you need to get out of your head. Here." He passed me the ball. "Let's try this."

I scrunched up my face as Derek moved behind me. "What are you doing?"

"Just look at the hoop."

Shrugging, I turned back and looked up at the net. Out of nowhere, two hands clapped over my eyes. "Hey!"

"Chill out," he said. "Now, I want you to take the shot."

"But I can't see anything."

"You don't need to see. You need to trust yourself. Now, take the shot."

"This is silly," I deadpanned.

"I'm the coach. You have to do everything I say. Take the shot."

I was seriously tempted to dispute that claim, but I had a feeling Derek would outlast me in any and every argument.

Taking a breath, I raised the ball and tried to see the hoop in my mind's eye. I threw it with all my might.

Clang! Thump. Thump.

Derek whistled. "Wow, Manning. Nice."

"Really?" I beamed. "I did it!"

He burst out laughing. "Nah. You totally missed. You weren't even close."

"Jerk." I ripped his hands off me as he howled.

"It's cool," he said between chuckling. "The point wasn't to make the shot. Let's try it again."

Over and over, Derek covered my eyes and made me shoot blindly at the hoop. I had no idea what the point was, but after a while, I started not to care.

"Ready, Manning?" he cried. "It's all you. Going for the world record of the most consecutive misses in a row. Your shots into the bleachers were particularly impressive."

I giggled. "Thank you. How did you learn this technique? Or are you making it up as you go?"

"Honestly, my dad taught me."

"He did?" I stopped, lowering my hands. "Why like this?"

"Believe it or not, when I was young there were some days when I wasn't the joy and delight you've come to know."

I was pretty sure Derek could feel my eyes roll beneath his fingers. "I think I can picture it."

"Anyway, I was a really angry kid. We went through a lot of nannies. One of them, on her way out, yelled at my parents and said things might be better if they spent more time with me. The next day, Dad put a ball in my hand and we started playing hoops.

"It wasn't great at first. I sucked and I tried to quit every day, but he wouldn't let me. Finally, he got tired of my whining, put his hands over my eyes, and said stop trying to be perfect and just have fun. Thus, blindfolded basketball was born. We'd have fun seeing how many we could get. Dad has sunk two, and with my skills, I'm still at zero. It makes regular basketball seem a lot easier."

I smiled. "That's sweet. Your dad sounds like a great guy."

His hands moved with his shrug. "He's decent. Now, stop stalling and throw."

I laughed. "Okay. Let's see if I can get the scoreboard again."

Blindly, I lifted my hands and threw the ball in the general direction of the hoop.

Thump. Whish.

"Oh, damn," Derek whispered. "You did it. Zeke, you made the shot."

"No way. Are you serious?" I grabbed his wrists and pulled them away. The ball rolled harmlessly down the court. "Don't mess with me."

"I'm not kidding, man," he said, excitement lacing his voice. "You actually sank it, and you didn't need math to do it."

A smile broke out on my face. The next thing I knew, I was squealing and jumping up and down. "I can't believe I did it!" I spun and threw my arms around him. "That is the coolest thing I've ever done. I can die now because I'm not going to top this."

He laughed, his body shaking in my hold. "You're so damn weird, Zeke, but I won't lie." He pulled back and met my eyes, grinning. "That was cool."

We stood there, smiling at each other, and for a moment, a feeling I couldn't describe filled me like bubbles and tried to lift me up. I wasn't hot or tired or sweaty. I was just here with Derek.

Bang!

"Time's up, Grayson."

We shot apart so fast I tripped over my heel and almost got acquainted with the floor.

"We're about to hold a battle," Singh continued as he strolled inside. "There are two tomorrow at four and four thirty, so come at five. You missed tryouts because of detention, but I want you on the team next semester. Keep practicing. Stay sharp."

"I will, Coach."

Hurriedly, we gathered our stuff and beat it out of there. We were quiet as we crossed the lawn and made for the dorms. Derek didn't speak until he set foot on the stairs.

"See you tomorrow afternoon."

"I'll be there."

He left without another word.

"OKAY, CLASS. PASS UP your worksheets, then open your history books," said Dawson. "Today, we're discussing Manifest Destiny and its impact on the expansion out west."

Ring. Ring.

"Just a moment," Dawson said as he moved back to his desk. "Tanner, collect the worksheets."

The boy rose while Dawson answered his phone. I reached into the hollow of my desk and pulled out my history book.

"Zeke."

I glanced up.

"You can put that away." He returned the phone to his cradle. "You're to report to Miss Val's office. Do you know the way?"

"Yes, I know." I stood and left.

I knew what this was about. Boys had been disappearing from my class all week to meet with Miss Val. It was time for our therapy session.

My feet carried me to her by memory. Visions of Zach punching me, Cameron threatening me, and Derek lying dead flooded my mind. I did not want to do this, but I knew Miss Val was just doing her job.

She seems like a smart lady. More than that, she is a lady. The boys might not notice my slipups, but trapped in a room with a woman trained to dig into your secrets was a recipe for getting found out. What do I do if she finds out Zeke is actually Zela?

I was no closer to answering that when I knocked on her door.

"Just a moment," I heard. Footsteps sounded on the other side of the door and then it swung open. She beamed. "Good morning, Zeke. Come in."

Not for the first time, I marveled at how beautiful she was. The woman wore pregnancy like a fertility goddess. The glow made her more radiant, and the waddle was just cute.

"Please, take a seat on the couch." She pointed away from her desk. "I like to keep it informal. Think of this as a conversation, instead of a therapy session."

The last time I was here, I didn't get the chance to take in what she'd done with the space. I could see the effort she made to make it cozy. There were pictures of her family everywhere—bright, happy, insanely attractive people smiling down at us instead of the shrine to accomplishments in Whittaker's office.

The corner she pointed to had a comfy blue couch and two matching armchairs, sitting on top of a shag, light green rug.

I went for the armchair instead of the couch. She said it wasn't therapy, but I knew how this went. I wasn't going to lie on the couch and spill my feelings.

If Miss Val had any thoughts on me taking the armchair, her face didn't give her away. She sat down on the couch like she was meant to be there all along.

I eyed her. "Where is your notepad? Or are you recording me?" I looked around. "I don't want to be recorded."

"There is no notepad or recorder. I told you. This is just a conversation." She leaned back, relaxing into the cushions as she placed her hands on her swollen belly. "So how are things going?"

"They're fine."

There was a pause, but I did not fill it with more.

"This is a big change for you," she said after a minute. "Transitioning from being homeschooled. Spending all this time away from your family. Navigating a unique way of schooling. How are you dealing with all of that?"

"It's great. I love it."

Another long silence. Through it, Miss Val didn't lose her smile.

"It seems you and Adam are getting close. I was happy to hear you're coming to stay with us this weekend."

"Yeah... me too." Slowly, I unclenched my hands. I could talk about this weekend. That was harmless. "I have to ask my mom first, but it would be nice to meet Adam's brother and sisters."

"They're excited to meet you too. We don't have anything big planned, because this one is coming any minute." She fondly rubbed her belly. "But I thought we could go to Adam's favorite restaurant, queue up a bunch of movies, and take a trip to the Promenade."

"That sounds great. Thank you for doing this." My shoulders loosened. "What is your town like? I've been all over the world, but when we're in the States, we never go far from Chesterfield."

"Evergreen is a lot like here, except..."

I relaxed as we talked. Miss Val wasn't tricking me. She let me lead the conversation and kept it chill. Maybe these mandatory sessions wouldn't be so bad.

"Okay, Zeke, our time is almost up."

"It is?" I glanced at the clock. Twenty-six minutes had passed without me noticing. "Wow. Thanks, Miss Val." I rose to leave.

"Before you go, there is something I wanted to ask you."

I slowly returned to my seat. "Ask me about what?"

"At the beginning of the year, your aunt asked me about having more sessions with you."

"You said Mom had to agree to that."

"Yes, and she has," Miss Val said calmly. "We spoke yesterday and decided you could benefit from it, but she has left it to us to determine how often we meet. I thought I would get your input."

My nails burrowed into the arms of the chair. "My input is I don't want to. I don't need more sessions."

Her gaze was unwavering. "Your mom and I had a long talk. She told me about the year you were six and you came to visit for Christmas."

My nails dug in so hard, they bent back and painfully pulled away from the skin.

Her words broke through the roaring in my ears. "—me what happened at the Chesterfield Mall."

"I don't want to talk about that," I whispered.

"It was a very traumatic experience. I cannot imagine what you went through. Your father—"

"Please, Miss Val." She blurred in my vision, becoming hazy and undefined as my eyes swam. "I can't talk about this."

"Zeke, I don't want to push you." Her voice softened. "I believe in letting people go at their own pace. Your mother is just worried because you've had her as a support system every day and now you have to spend so much time apart. She wants to know you're okay."

"I'm fine."

"Are you?" I jumped when a hand curled around mine and gently pried it off. "I know the Elite boys have been targeting you."

I jerked my head up in surprise. "Adam—"

"No," she said firmly. "He did not tell me anything. I get notified every time a battle goes through so I can keep track of how many a student is in during a semester. You've had the most and it's been a month. I can see you're being targeted and I want you to know I'm here for you." She squeezed my hand. "I'm here if you want to talk about... anything."

It took me a while, but I nodded. "I know." I tugged my hand free. "Can I go now?"

"Yes, you can. We'll meet once every two weeks going forward."

I didn't argue. It was Mom who got me into this and I didn't know why. I told her I was fine. Why didn't she believe me? Seeing Miss Val wouldn't make things right. I was doing that on my own. I just had to get close to Derek, then everything would be okay.

"ARE YOU OKAY?"

"I'm fine." I tugged the marker from his hand. "Why?"

"You get all quiet when something is bothering you."

"Quiet? You act like I run my mouth all the time."

"You do."

I promptly flung the marker at Adam's head.

He laughingly ducked it. "I'm serious. What's wrong? Is Derek giving you a hard time?"

"No." I thought back to the day before and us laughing when the ball sailed back and almost bashed in my nose. "He's been nice. I'm learning a lot from him."

"Landon tossing you around like a sack of feathers?"

I chuckled. "Yes, actually. The guy said I'd be his practice dummy and he wasn't kidding. He's giving me a lot of tips, but usually while he's throwing and flipping me around." I pressed my hand to my warm cheek. "At least soccer is a lot less physical."

Landon and I had been practicing together for only a few days, but I was feeling way more confident than I did at the start of the week.

"Then what is it?" Adam pressed.

Sighing, I looked away. We were in the multipurpose room for the Stand Up meeting. The first official game of the year was next week and we were making our signs for the protest. People were scattered around the room, working in groups. Most of those groups were girls.

It made sense since Melody had an easier time recruiting from the girls' side than she did ours, but it was a bit uneven having twenty-two girls, five guys, and me.

I peeked at Cameron through my lashes. *And him.*

He hadn't spoken to me since the hallway, but he did come to the meeting like the dutiful boyfriend and sat at Melody's table handing her glitter and markers with a smile on his face.

In no universe does this guy want to get rid of the battle system. How good of an actor is he?

"Psst, Zeke," Adam hissed. "She's coming."

I tore my eyes off of him, grabbed the poster, and flipped it over just in time. Mrs. Gold stepped up to our table and peered over Adam's shoulder.

"Oooh. Very nice," she said. "What a cute drawing of an owl."

We thanked her and she moved on to another group. Only when she took her place at the table in front of the room and went back to her grading did we relax.

It was interesting organizing a protest under the nose of our advisor, but Melody was so formidable because she was smart. She organized a very real fundraiser for the local nonprofit that rescued and rehabilitated animals in our area. We had the signs for that on one side and the protest signs on the other.

"Did I tell you that Owen and Justin are coming over tomorrow? We're going to hit the Promenade and see a movie."

"Love it. I've been dying to see that murder mystery."

"Owen wants to see the horror movie."

"Owen wants me to watch through the cracks in my fingers."

He busted up. "Okay. No horror movies."

We finished up with both sides of the poster, said bye to Melody, and then headed out. The end of the school week brought all the joy it usually did. We passed by boys on their way out and those staying in. Miss Val was waiting for us outside her office and together we pushed through the grand doors and stepped out into the chilly autumn afternoon.

October had been good to Breakbattle. The trees were shedding their red and gold leaves and scattering them all over the lawn. They looked like colorful sprinkles on a bed of green icing.

A football game had started near the gates. Boys in their weekend uniform of a loose cotton shirt with their class letters on the front and back, ran all over the place. Breakbattle wanted us to always know where we belonged.

The ride to the town of Evergreen wasn't long. Soon, the forest cleared and revealed grass. Lots and lots of grass and hills and more grass. That wasn't the sight to see. No, what made me press my nose to the mirror were the grand mansions set way back in the middle of their massive acres, and atop their hills.

"Whoa," I whispered. "And you said this place was a dump, Adam."

"Total dump. Barely livable. We want to move, don't we, Mom?"

"It's a wonder we haven't already," Miss Val threw in. "Can't stand the place."

The car filled with giggles and my tension eased. I was a little worried about being around Miss Val after our session, but she seemed perfectly happy to carry on like normal.

"Miss Val?"

"Call me Val, Zeke. We're not in school."

"Val," I corrected. "Did you grow up here?"

"No. Adam and I are from a town called Wakefield..."

Val told me her story as we turned off the road and stopped in front of iron gates. The guard, yes guard, let us in at the sight of her and they opened on a magnificent manor the likes of which I had only seen on guided tours.

The car pulled up to the mansion and Val and Adam hopped out like it was no big deal. I needed a few more seconds of gawking.

Eventually, I gathered my stuff and climbed out of the car. Adam was waiting for me on the top steps and together the both of us followed Val inside.

"You can put your shoes there." Adam pointed out the shoe rack. "And there are slippers in that one if you want."

"Great." I bent to take off my sneakers.

"Oh, Zeke," Val spoke up. "This is my daughter, Esme. She's seven. Esme, come say hi."

I lifted my head and a young girl in a silver dress stepped into the entrance. Her resemblance to Val was so strong, she didn't need to tell me she was her daughter. The only difference between them was the thick, black waterfall that ran down Esme's shoulders in place of Val's wavy chestnut locks—those, and her eyes. Her eyes pierced me as Esme came over.

"Hi, Esme." I straightened and held out my hand. "Nice to meet you. I'm Zeke."

"You're Zeke?"

"Yeah. That's me."

"Adam's my best friend."

"What?"

Her adorable face crumpled into a frown so fast, I didn't have time to react. "He's mine!"

"Ow!" Pain blossomed in my leg sharp and vicious. I doubled over, clutching my shin.

"Esme Marie Lennox!"

Esme burst into wails and ran from the room, her mom waddling fast on her heels.

"You come back here right now, young lady. I told you no more kicking!"

A thump made me turn my head to find Adam rolling on the floor, laughing as tears ran down his cheeks.

"What was that?!" I cried.

"I'm s-sorry! She's a little possessive."

"A little? I'm going to have a limp!"

That only set him off again. Kissing my teeth, I grabbed my stuff and left him on the floor.

Thankfully, the visit improved from there. Adam found me in the living room, assured me she kicks all his friends, and then took me to meet the rest of the family. His dads I knew, but I also got to meet his grandma Olivia and grandma Caroline.

Grandma Caroline was lying out on the porch with two snoozing three-year-olds on her chest. I wasn't rude enough to ask, but from the thick head of hair and brown shade to their skin, I guessed this little boy and girl were Val and Maverick's kids.

"Hello, Zeke," Caroline greeted me. "I'm pinned down at the moment, but once I get these little ones to bed, we're taking our dinner and enjoying it in front of the screen. I hope you like old movies."

"I love them."

She looked over at Adam. "I like this friend of yours, love. Bring him around more often."

He laughed as he bent to pick up his brother. He pecked her cheek on the way up. "I will, Grandma."

They're so sweet.

That was the word to describe this family: sweet.

My family was a bunch of different, strong personalities thrown together and doing their best to make it work, but these eleven people made loving each other look so effortless. I had such a great time with them when Mom came to pick me up Sunday morning, I almost forgave her for making me take extra sessions with Miss Val.

Almost.

Mom and I made the trip back to Chesterfield in silence. Well, the radio was on and music poured between us the entire time, but otherwise, we did not speak. My mom did not stand disrespect in any shape or form, so I kept my feelings about what she did inside.

She must have sensed them though because partway through the journey, she reached over and took my hand. Mom did not say anything or look away from the road. She just held me as I fought not to cry.

"THANK YOU, MRS. PETERSON."

"Not at all, Zeke." She put her hand on my shoulder as we walked toward the door. "See you at the game."

"Can't wait."

I waved and then left her classroom. It had been a week since our club meeting and my trip to Adam's house.

There was a skip in my step as I hurried down the stairs. Everything was falling into place. Between Derek and Landon, I was getting better and better every day. Landon said as much the day before. As for history, I didn't know what the next test would bring, but I had been studying, quizzing, and taking notes constantly. I was coming for my stuff.

Adam and the rest of Stand Up were waiting for me in our meeting place by the pool. Sporting events were one of the rare occasions when the boys and girls were allowed to mix which made it the perfect time for our protest. Everyone would be there from the students to the principal. We would not be ignored.

Melody rested the stack of posters against the building. "Everyone, grab yours. Remember, we're waiting until just before the game starts and then we'll go in with our signs up. Make sure they all get a good look as you take your seat like nothing's up. Got it?"

"Got it," we replied.

We stepped up to get our posters and admire each other's handiwork. Some of the slogans people came up with were quite clever.

Letter Grades are for Tests, Not People.

Encourage Bonds Over Battles.

Adam and I went simple with End the Class and Battle System.

"Hold on. What's this?" Melody was frowning at her poster. "I didn't put this here."

"What's up?" I asked.

She turned it around and pointed to a small sticker in the corner. "Where did this come from?"

"I've got one too."

"Me too."

"Yeah. There's a sticker on mine."

I scanned mine as everyone chimed in and there it was. A tiny upside-down sticker of an A. I scrunched up my face. "You know it kind of looks like..."

"Like what?" Melody asked when I trailed off.

"It looks like a math symbol," I finished. "The symbol looks like an upside-down A and it means 'for all.'"

"For all?" she repeated. "For all. Actually... I like that. That's what we're about. We're doing this for all of us." She smiled. "Did one of you do this? Did you make this sticker for our group?"

Looking around, everyone shook their heads.

Beep. Beep.

"That's my alarm," she said. "We can figure it out later. It's time to go in."

Adam and I shared a look as we fell in line. Silent protest or not, there was a chance there could be fallout from this.

One by one, we entered the rush and roar of the stadium. Breakbattle didn't have cheerleaders, but that didn't stop people from chanting, shouting, and jumping in the stands, getting ready for our championship team to come out led by Cameron Dupre. We were going up against a team from the local high school, Chesterfield.

As we neared our bleachers, Adam moved to my other side to grab one corner and together we lifted the sign high. I watched their faces as people stopped chanting and read our posters. It didn't happen all at once, but the noise level died as shock struck people silent. Mrs. Argyle's jaw literally dropped.

Our side of the room was split by boys and girls and then the rows were sectioned by class. The Elite were on the bottom while Adam and I climbed the stairs to the very top where Tanner and Nico gaped at us.

"What the hell are you two doing?" Tanner hissed. "You trying to get suspended?"

"We're trying to end the system," I said as we slid in next to him. "It's about time Whittaker and Argyle knew how the students truly felt."

It took a minute for the Chesterfield kids to read our signs. When they did, a true hush descended on the room. The other school lowered their banners and noisemakers like they didn't know what to do.

Eeeeeeppp!

Audio feedback cut through the room. "All right, Chesterfield! Breakbattle! Let's get this game started!" The MC forced a laugh. "Get that energy up, people, because here they come!"

The basketball teams jogged out onto the court to a smattering of applause. I wasn't nearly so worried about that as I was about Whittaker and Argyle. The two were out of their seats and bearing down on Melody fast.

"Shit," I heard Adam say.

Our eyes were glued on them. We couldn't see Melody's face, but we could see Argyle's and Whittaker's and they were not happy. After a brief back and forth, Melody stepped away from the bench and followed Whittaker out the door. She displayed her sign proudly until he took it out of her hands.

It was our turn next.

Argyle stood before the stairs and mimed that she wanted us all to come down. None of us moved. Behind her, the game was getting underway.

Argyle looked us dead in the eyes and leveled two fingers at us. Her message was clear.

We held firm until our teachers rose from their seats. Mr. Jessop got Owen out and sent him down to the vice principal. Mr. Dawson came for us.

"Boys," he began. His tone was low and even. "I believe Mrs. Argyle wants you."

"We're not doing anything wrong," Adam spoke up. "We have a right to protest."

He gave us an amused grin. "And I promise you won't be arrested, but she's asked you to come down and I suggest you do before—"

Crack!

Shouts tore through the room followed by piercing screams. The poster slipped out of our hands as I whipped around. The Elite boys were on the floor, scattered around and on top of them was the splintered wreck that used to be their bench.

Argyle forgot all about us. She and the other teachers ran to their aid as groaning from shock and pain, they struggled to untangle themselves from each other. Landon clutched the back of his head as he staggered to his feet.

"Holy hell," Nico breathed. "How does that happen?"

"I hope they're okay," Adam whispered, but still it echoed in the space.

The entire room fell silent except worried teachers asking the boys if they were all right. The game had come to a dead halt, players just standing in the middle of the court.

I stepped around Adam. My chest was tight as I clambered down the stairs and took in the full sight.

"How does this happen?"

One of the teachers escorted the Elites to the nurse while the others carefully, but quickly evacuated the stands.

The game was over.

"I'VE NEVER SEEN ANYTHING like that."

The weekend had come and gone, but the accident at the game was the only topic of conversation on Monday morning.

Tanner grabbed a tray and joined the line. "I thought these gyms were state of the art and paid for with the money they hold back from the Fs. How do bleachers just break like that?"

"What if ours had?" Nico spoke up from behind me. "We had a much bigger drop."

I did not like that thought at all.

"I heard they were all okay," Adam spoke up. "Mom talked to the nurse and said there were just a few scratches and head bumps."

"That's a relief," I said.

We got our food and took it to our usual table where Justin and Owen were waiting. They started the conversation up again the minute we sat down.

"I thought the biggest thing that would happen at the game was our protest," Owen said.

"I still can't believe you guys did that," said Justin. "What do you think Whittaker is going to do?"

"Something tells me we're about to find out."

Our heads moved as if on a swivel. Across the cafeteria, Whittaker, Argyle, Miss Val, Mr. Orlov, Mr. Dawson, and a couple of other teachers walked inside and made for the head table. It was there, always sitting empty and waiting for the day they would decide to have a meal with us. Apparently, that day was today.

Whittaker claimed the seat in the middle while the others fanned out around him. They fell into conversation while the food staff brought them plates of food, but as for the rest of the room, the noise dropped to a dull roar.

We tried to get back into regular conversation. It was difficult with us sneaking glances at the head table every five seconds.

"Guys, look," Justin hissed. "Whittaker is standing up."

I dropped my sausage and spun around. Whittaker was on his feet, taking his time as he smoothed down his suit and fixed his cuffs.

"Ladies and gentlemen, quiet please." He needn't have said that. The room was quiet as a graveyard. "I need to speak with you about the incident at the basketball game. People were brought in and assessed how the accident could have happened and they determined... that it was not an accident."

Gasps went up through the cafeteria, mine was one of them. *Not an accident? How was that possible?*

"The Elite rows and *only* the Elite rows were sabotaged so that the wood would buckle under the stress." Whittaker scanned the crowd with narrowed eyes. "We discovered that the same damage was done to the girls' side. It was a miracle that theirs did not collapse before we evacuated.

"No one was seriously injured, and it's possible that the person or persons who did this did not think anyone would be hurt. This could have been intended as an extremely misguided prank, but the fact remains, what was done was a gross assault on your fellow students. Whoever did this will be found and punished, but the severity of that punishment relies on if you step forward willingly or if we are forced to suss out the responsible party ourselves. Am I understood?"

"Yes, sir," we chorused.

He acknowledged our response with a sharp nod and took his seat. I thought that was it until Argyle stood up.

"In that vein," she said, "every member of the student organization, Stand Up, is to stay behind after breakfast. Do not try to sneak out. I have the list of all the members." With that, she sat down.

We traded glances around the table. What were we supposed to do? Were we really going to get in trouble for silently holding up a sign?

Ding! Ding!

"Good luck, guys," Justin said as he gathered his tray. "I'll catch you up at lunch."

I swallowed as I looked past him to the stormy expressions on Whittaker and Argyle's faces.

If we make it to lunch.

"All of you," Whittaker announced, "move to these tables in the front."

We got up and did as he asked. Melody took a seat right in front of Whittaker. Her face was blank as she looked him in the eye.

"Before we begin," the principal said, "is there something you want to tell me?"

The soft sound of someone clearing their throat drew our eyes. Melody got to her feet. "Sir, if you're asking if we're responsible for the attack on the Elites, the answer is no. I was sitting on that bench too."

Mr. Orlov shot out of his seat. "Are we to believe the timing of your protest and the attack were just a coincidence?"

"Yes."

"Now, listen here—"

"Arthur," Argyle cut in. "Let us handle this."

Melody stepped forward. "We didn't do this, Mrs. Argyle. Our protest was peaceful. All we did and all we planned to do was hold up our signs. You believe us, don't you?"

"We do." My eyes snapped to Miss Val. "My son would not be a part of any attack against other students," she continued.

"Just like he wouldn't be a part of a protest against the school and everything it's built on," Orlov shot back.

Miss Val shook her head. "No, he would be a part of that. He told me as much."

"So you knew!"

"Before Friday, I did not know, but I do now. He has been honest about his involvement in the protest and all the other students are here facing up to it as well. I don't believe they would do so if they sabotaged the bleachers."

The club members chimed in, agreeing with her.

"I didn't hurt anyone."

"I would never do that."

"Melody was on the bench too. Why would she sit if she knew?"

"We're not crazy."

"Okay, okay. Settle down." Whittaker repeated himself a few times before he got silence. "We don't have proof that anyone here is responsible for the sabotage, so we won't be punishing you for that."

"But, sir!" Orlov cried.

"However," he plowed on. "We do know you embarrassed the school in front of guests and held a protest without permission. New students tend to have strong feelings against the system. This is new to all of you. You don't know how to handle the pressure, and as children, your first instinct is to run from what can make you stronger. I know and I understand this."

A smile spread across his lips. "Over time, you will see the battle system is the best thing for you. It will help you grow into the strong, talented individuals you are destined to become, and it is the system that will get you there. That is why no matter how many signs you make or how much you protest; the system will not be changed."

He stood and faced us down. "This is what Breakbattle is and will always be. If you do not like it, you have the option to transfer to another high school. In the meantime, everyone here will receive two weeks' detention."

People groaned, but were quickly silenced by the raising of his hand.

"I will allow this club to remain open," he went on, "because I believe you can do good in the community, but you will be on probation. If there is one more protest against this school, Stand Up will be shut down. Is that clear?"

"Yes, sir," we replied.

"Now, get to class."

Quietly, we filed out and broke apart to go to our classes.

"I can't believe someone sabotaged the benches," Adam said, mostly to himself. "What if Melody's had snapped? Who would do that?"

"Could it have been a prank?"

"Maybe. I just hope nothing like that happens again."

"Me too."

We went back to class and were immediately bombarded with questions. Things didn't settle down until Mr. Dawson came back and started the lesson.

I got through the day, and detention, and was finally let out at three o'clock. I didn't waste time in rushing back to the dorm and climbing the stairs to the very top.

An Elite boy stepped out of his room just as I walked in. He was wearing a jersey and gym shorts that told of where he was going. I tensed as he passed by me, but he didn't look in my direction.

I went to Derek's dorm and knocked.

"Who is it?"

"It's me."

I heard shuffling on the other side of the door and then it opened. "What do you want?"

"I came to see if you were okay," I said, although looking at him I saw there wasn't a scratch on him. "I missed you at breakfast and lunch."

He stepped back and I took that as a sign I could come in. I went for his desk chair and pushed it next to the bed.

"Came to see if I was okay?" he repeated. "What? Were you worried about me?"

"Yes."

His mocking smile slipped. "Are you for real?"

"Yes, I'm for real. Why wouldn't I be worried about you? You're my friend."

Derek sat down next to me, giving me a look I couldn't read.

"I also wanted to make sure you knew Stand Up had nothing to do with the bench collapsing," I went on. "I realized that some people might think we did, but I would never be a part of anything to hurt you or the other guys. Whoever did that was messed up."

"Whoever did that better watch out," he corrected. "Santiago and Heath were spitting mad. Cameron swore they were going to find who did it and dole out their own punishment."

I sighed. "Are traditional schools always like this?"

"Yeah. Pretty much."

Despite myself, I laughed. "I'm just glad you're okay."

He smiled back at me for a moment, then it faded. He looked away. "You should go. The court is closed while they fix the gym so we can't practice."

"But I don't have to leave so soon," I said as he got up. "I was hoping we could hang out."

"I've got a test to study for." Derek went to the door and peeked out. "The hallway is clear. See you around, man."

Confused, I picked myself up and walked out. Derek closed the door before I could turn around. I tried not to let his dismissal get to me as the night wore on, but when he walked past our table for his harem of girls, I couldn't fight a niggle of sadness. Every time I thought I was getting close to him; I'd blink and he'd be even further away.

The next morning, I woke early and snuck away to the showers. I would say it was a miracle I had never been caught in here, but it was down to the simple fact that no one was up this early. No one except one guy.

Michael was a graceful figure gliding around the track when I approached. I paused in front of the bleachers and watched him. The sun hadn't made it to our side of the world yet, but it was casting a soft, orange glow on the horizon to say it was on its way. There was no one else around but us. It was quiet, peaceful... perfect.

Michael slowed down when he caught sight of me. "What are you doing here?"

"I came to run."

"I like to run alone."

I shrugged. "It's not like I'll be running next to you. I can't keep up." I turned around and propped my foot on the bench. "Ignore me."

There was silence for a moment while I began to stretch, then I caught the sounds of his shoes smacking against the track.

To get on the same level as the Elite, I needed to put in the hours. I discovered a love of running during orientation and it was a great way to keep in shape. That Michael was here every day was an added bonus.

I began a light jog around the track, easing into it. I also discovered a crush on Michael during orientation, but it had been weird between the two of us to say the least. He hadn't spoken to me outside of our battles to take my things. Zach didn't have to speak; it was obvious he was enjoying himself. Landon expressed regret over what he had to do, but Cole and Michael said nothing.

Although, from watching them over the last month, it didn't look like they spoke to anyone else other than each other and their coaches. It was like nothing else existed outside of their mission to make it to the Olympics.

The burn crept into my lungs as I finished the first lap. I slowed my pace a bit and breathed through it.

"Don't quit."

"What?"

Michael pulled out ahead of me. A light sheen of sweat clung to his body, but he didn't look winded. "Why are you slowing down? You basically walked around the track. Push yourself. You can do it."

I cracked a smile. "I thought you were ignoring me."

To my surprise, he smiled back. "Keep pace with me. I'll slow it down for you."

Michael picked up speed as I considered my options. *It would be nice to hang with him again. Even if it half kills me to keep pace with him at any speed.*

Going for it, I picked up my feet and fell in beside him. Together we did one lap around the track, and then two. The sun crested over the horizon by the time I called it quits. I veered off for the bleachers and noticed right away that he did too.

"I'm going to come back tomorrow," I said. "I can come at a later time if you want to be alone."

"Nah. Don't bother with that. I don't own the track." He plopped down and reached for the water bottle beneath the bench. "Besides, someone has to make sure you don't half-ass it out there."

I couldn't be sure, but I had a feeling this was Michael's way of apologizing. The smile that thought brought me would have scared him off, so I bit my lip to hold it back.

"Okay. I'll see you tomorrow."

I practically floated back to the dorm. It was still early enough that I was able to grab a quick shower and rinse off my run before meeting Adam as he woke up. He got ready and then we headed out for breakfast.

"So you're training and getting better at sports every day," said Adam. "That was step one. When does step two start?"

I passed him a tray and picked up one for myself. "I'm very happy you asked that because it starts today."

"Today?" he said under his breath. He peered around. "Are you going to do it here?"

"I have to. Today is the last day."

"Then do it now." He pointed across the room with his chin. "He's here. Go, I'll get your food for you."

Taking a deep breath, I set off across the cafeteria for a table near the head. The boys were laughing and goofing off, throwing their grapes at each other and attempting to catch them in their mouths. One sailed over his head and bounced off his chest.

He twisted around. "Oh. Sorry about that."

"It's fine. Are you Miles Harmon?"

"Yeah. Why?"

"Miles Harmon, I challenge you to a battle."

The grape throwing ceased immediately. The boys all gaped at me. Miles's mouth hung wider than them all. "You? Challenge me?" He thumped his chest. "Did you not see I'm in the B Class?"

"I know what class you're in," I said calmly. "I challenge you in history for your spot in the Archimedean Club."

"The Archimedean Club?" He barked a laugh. "Now I know you're joking. That club is for advanced mathematics, dude. There's a reason they don't let Fs in. Stop messing around and walk away."

I didn't move. "Does that mean you're refusing the battle?"

His brows snapped together in a frown. "I'm not refusing. I'm saving you the embarrassment of losing. Take the challenge back."

"I'm not taking it back. You don't need to worry about embarrassing me. I've lost eight battles already. So you should accept now or I'm going to start thinking it's you who is afraid of losing."

Miles scowled. "Fine," he snapped. "We'll make it official after breakfast."

"Perfect."

I flashed Adam a thumbs-up as I approached our table. Now for the hard part.

Miles chose soccer for the physical test and we got it approved and scheduled for Thursday. I didn't believe it was possible to study history harder than I already was, but I proved myself wrong. I crammed my mind with so many history facts they were spilling out of my ears.

"Why did you choose history?" Tanner asked.

Thursday had come and the four of us were spending the last hour before the battle helping me study.

"Do you want to lose?"

"No, I don't. I chose history again because I have a theory. If it works out, I'll get into the Archimedean Club."

"Still sounds like losing to me. We don't study enough during school? Why would you join a club where you'd have to study even more?"

"I like math," I protested. "It'll be fun."

He rolled his eyes. "How are we friends?"

"Are you helping me or not?

"Alright. Fine." Tanner picked up his textbook and flipped through the pages. "What did the War of 1812...?"

The guys stuck around until Mr. Dawson walked in with Miles and his teacher on his heels.

"You both know the routine by now," Dawson said. "You'll have thirty minutes to write a short essay. Flip over your papers when I say so."

Dawson rested the sheet on my desk and I took a minute to cross all my fingers and toes. I was hanging this battle on a guess. If I was wrong, my entire plan would fall apart.

"You may begin."

I quickly flipped over the paper and read the question.
I smiled.

FWEEET!

"That's time!"

Miles and I backed away from the ball and jogged off the field.

"Good game," I called at his back.

He scoffed. "We tied, F, and everyone knows you suck at history. You lost this battle. I told you not to waste my time." He snatched up his stuff and marched off as Adam handed me my water bottle.

"Your plan," Adam said. "Did it work?"

"We'll find out tomorrow."

The next morning, I went in early to class. I tried to sit still in the dorm, waiting for Adam to wake up, but nervous energy finally propelled me out of bed. I had to know if I won.

Mr. Dawson looked up when I burst in. "Zeke. Can't say I wasn't expecting you."

"Do you have the results?" I marched up to him and planted my hands on his desk. "Did I win the battle?"

He let out a sigh. "I'm afraid I have bad news, Zeke."

My heart sank to the pit of my gut. "I lost again? But I knew the answer to the history question. I thought I did well."

Dawson came around the desk and clapped a hand on my shoulder. "The bad news is you'll be stuck in a math club once a week when you could be having a life."

I blinked as his words penetrated. "Stuck in a math... Are you saying I won? I won?!"

A smile split his face. "Your history essay was incredibly detailed and informative. You even threw in a few points that are not in your textbook." He squeezed my shoulder. "I've been very impressed with the hard work you've put in over the weeks. So impressed that it is clear to me I owe you an apology. I had begun to see my students as no more than the letter on their uniforms. You, all of you, have so much potential and I'm excited to help you reach it."

"Oh, Mr. Dawson, this is— This is—" I squealed and threw my arms around him. "This is amazing! Thank you! Thank you!"

"Whoa, Zeke." Dawson grabbed my arms and peeled me off. "You can't hug your teacher in an empty classroom. That's how rumors start." He set me a respectable distance away. "But you've done well. The Archimedean Club is lucky to have you."

"Thank you."

I went to my desk to wait for class to start. All day I tried and failed to contain my excitement. Not only were things going smoothly, but I was finally going to learn the math I came here to learn.

The next day after classes let out, I climbed the steps to the sixth floor with my head held high. I kept my chin up as I stepped into Mrs. Peterson's classroom. If only I had a camera to snap the look on Santiago's face when he saw me.

"Zeke, there you are." Peterson came to me and put her arm around my shoulder. "I was so thrilled when I heard the news. I can't wait to work with you." She looked out at the class. "Did you hear that, everyone? This is our new and final member of Archimedean Club."

Santiago's face when she said that would have made for another great picture. Apparently, he could make another expression besides blank or bored.

"I'm sure you'll make him feel welcome." She patted my arm. "Take any free seat."

I zeroed in on one and walked over without hesitation. "Hey, Cole."

I once described Cole as softer, smoother, which was a strange description for someone who scowled as much as he did.

"What are you doing?"

"I'm sitting down." I pulled out the chair and plopped my butt in it to illustrate my point.

"That's not what I'm talking about." His eyes flicked over my shoulder. "Cameron is going to lose his mind when he finds out you got into this club. I bet Santi's texting him right now."

I peered over my shoulder. Santiago was on his phone and he was not looking happy. "Why should either of them care? It's none of their business."

"They've made you their business, and because of that, I've got to spend all my time in stupid battles for shit I don't want. The first swim meet is next semester and Coach Nelson is putting together the team that will represent us now. I'm getting that spot, not Moon."

"Can't you both get a spot? You shouldn't see members of your own team as competition."

He shook his head. "Even after everything, you're still this naïve. Scouts come to our games all the time and they don't take *teams*. They take the best. I will be the best."

I heaved a sigh. "Even after everything, you're still this intense. I don't want to stop you from being the best. I think it's cool you want to represent in the Olympics and I hope you make it happen. You're really talented."

"I— But you— He—" Cole tripped over his tongue. His expression was a mix of annoyed and confused as though he didn't know what to do with my sudden compliments. "Look, the point is Cam won't let this go. He's going to come for you by making *us* come for you."

"You know what that sounds like?"

"What?"

"It sounds like we have a common enemy."

I turned away as Mrs. Peterson booted up her smartboard. "Good afternoon, members. Let's start with our warm-up. The first person to answer this question, gets to push the buzzer during our math relay. A coveted prize."

I won that coveted prize. Peterson divided the class into two groups and had one person from each race to the board and attempt to solve the problem as fast as they could. It was also a challenge for the buzzer person, because I had to follow and figure out the right answer to buzz the winner. It was the most fun I've had at this school since I got here.

An hour later, Mrs. Peterson called time. Cole and I went to the desk to get our things.

"You're not terrible."

My hands stilled. "Cole Reed, was that a compliment?"

"It was barely one," he replied. I picked up a hint of amusement in his tone. "Nice to see you earned your title as human calculator. I don't mess with losers."

I zipped up my backpack. "But you mess with me."

He grabbed his bag and sidestepped me. "I didn't say that."

I was right on his heels. "You like me."

"Shut up."

"You want to be my friend."

Cole made a strangled noise.

Oh my goodness. Was that... a laugh?

"I swear you're the weirdest guy I've ever met."

"Then why do you want to be friends with me so badly?"

Cole let out another noise. This time I was sure it was a laugh.

The two of us walked out of Peterson's class. I made it three steps before he was on me.

"Zeke, I challenge you to a battle in history."

I backed up and bumped into a hard chest. Twisting around, I found Santi directly behind me. His face was blank again. Arms crossed, he looked down at me with eyes I couldn't read and it unsettled me worse than his anger.

I turned back to Zach and his smirk. A crowd had formed behind him and Cameron stood front and center. His fury wasn't masked.

"A battle for what?" I asked.

"For your spot in the Archimedean Club."

"No."

"No?" He smiled wider. "Then you'll lose a whole letter grade, idiot, and I'll just keep challenging you."

"You can try but you'd be wasting your time. Mrs. Peterson finalized the club roster today. I'm a member for the rest of the semester. No one can battle for my spot."

Zach's smirk twitched. "But—"

A hand seized his shoulder and shoved him aside. "Santi, is that true?" Cameron demanded.

"It can't be."

His presence suddenly disappeared and the other sophomore Elites took his place, closing me in. I held Cameron's gaze without flinching. There were too many teachers up here for them to try something.

Cameron's glare poured through me and burned from the inside out. I had never been faced with someone who disliked me as much as he did. It was even worse that I had done nothing to deserve it. Whatever was happening between us, I could see in his eyes that he would not let it end until he got a result I wouldn't like.

So I'll end it first.

"It's true." Santi's voice broke through our staredown. "The homeschooler stays."

"What? Move!" Cameron roughly knocked me to the side as he stormed into Peterson's class.

I turned my attention on Zach. "There you have it. Take the challenge back."

His lips twisted. "I'm not taking anything back. There's still plenty of stuff for us to get our hands on. We haven't gotten to your towels, clothes, toothbrush. Peterson will run your foul-smelling ass out of the club all on her own."

I clenched my fists as a pit lodged in my throat. Zach had become so awful. To think I once believed this guy could be my friend.

"Make your challenge, then, and if I win, I get my sheets back."

He leaned in close. "You won't win." I wrinkled my nose as his stale breath washed over me. "History it is, and I'll take that towel."

And then it began.

Weeks and weeks of battles for whatever they could get their hands on. Cameron liked Zach's idea too much and he sent him, Cole, Landon, and Michael after every single item I owned. The week Zach got my deodorant was the worst.

He went out of his way to track me down after his win, even going so far as to wait for me outside of class. He followed me around, gagging on my smell, and the other boys found it so funny they joined in.

It was everything in me not to cry when I walked into the lunchroom and the boys gave me a wide berth, even going so far as to vacate the tables around me when I sat down.

Adam, Tanner, Nico, Justin, Owen, and Melody had my back. They were ruthless about telling off the assholes who tried to get in my face, and every one of them offered to give me their deodorant. I refused, making do with frequent trips to the bathroom to clean myself off. I would not let Cameron or Zach think they were getting to me.

I held my resolve for three days until Cole placed something on my lap in the middle of Archimedean Club.

"What's this?" I peeked down and found a stick of deodorant on my lap. I closed my hand over it to give it back, then the next thing I knew I was slipping it into my backpack. "Thank you."

"I did it for me. I'm the one who has to sit next to you."

I smiled despite his reply. "I knew you liked me."

He kept his gaze straight ahead, but I could swear I peeked a smile.

The gesture was sweet, but it was the next day that the staff visited us at breakfast and Whittaker announced that battles could no longer be held for "articles of daily living." No more toiletries, no clothes, no towels, no accessories.

Every F student in the room cheered.

There were rough losses, but as time passed, there were wins too. I studied history more than I ever had in my life and it was bound to pay off. With Derek, Michael, and Landon's training, I began closing the gap in the physical tests. I got my sheets back, then my chair, then my mattress pad, and then my pillows. Cameron looked madder and madder every day.

"He's been so weird lately," Melody said. She picked at her lasagna. "He's always busy, never has time to hang out, and blows me off to eat with his friends." She glanced over to where Cameron sat huddled with Heath and Santiago. "He's like a completely different guy."

"I'm sorry," I said. "You deserve better than that."

"I do," she agreed. "He better figure that out soon."

Justin spoke up. "Maybe he's stressed about finals. I've used all my library time slots this week and I still feel like I don't know anything."

Owen shook his head. "You're always convinced you're going to fail and then you walk out with an A. You know everyone else hates people like you?"

"For sure, man," Tanner said. "The worst."

We laughed and Justin soon joined in. "You're right. It'll be fine. It will be fine, right?"

Owen stood. "Okay. Let's go back to your dorm and you can spiral there. I'll test you on bio if you want."

"Thanks, Owen."

They left and then it was down to just the F kids when Melody went to find her friends. Soon we finished eating and picked up our trays.

"I'm not worried," said Tanner. "I've learned so much history because of Zeke that I've got that sewn up. It's just algebra and biology, but we've been studying those like crazy."

"True," said Nico. He dumped his tray and led the way out of the cafeteria. "Finals won't be so—" Nico ground to a stop. The three of us passed through the doors but didn't make it any further than him.

Cameron, Santiago, Heath, and the rest of Cameron's crew were lined up, blocking us from getting through.

I stepped in front of Nico. "What now, Cameron?" I kissed my teeth. "Why won't you give it a rest?"

"I could have. I wanted to, but you"—he closed the distance between us—"wouldn't let it be. You knew what you were doing when you joined our math club. You refuse to learn your place but that's okay. I've got plenty of time and people to waste it for me." He threw out his hands. "I'll just keep sending Landon, Michael, and the rest after you until you and Moon make up for what you did during orientation."

My eyes bugged. "Us make it up to you?"

For a moment, he lost his mocking smirk. "We got detention because of you. Coach put me on probation and my dad went insane. All because you two were too stupid to know you were being played.

"If you apologize in front of everyone and tell them you made it all up, plus do a few other things for us, all of this stops. No one in the Elite Class will mess with you again."

He moved back, molding into his gang. "You have until to-morrow morning. If you both get up in front of the cafeteria and say you're sorry, we'll take it that we have a deal. I'm sure you'll make the right choice."

The five of them turned their backs on us. Cameron grew fuzzy around the edges. Fury I had only felt once before crept into my vision and blotted everything out.

After everything he had done to me, he thought I should give him an apology? He thinks he has a right to be mad at us because we didn't fall for his sick manipulation?

"I made my choice." The sentence made Cameron stop in his tracks. It took me a few seconds to realize it came from me. "We don't have to wait until tomorrow. I'll tell you what I'm going to do right now."

A hand grasped my shoulder as he faced me. "What are you doing, Zeke?" Adam asked.

"What am I doing?" I lifted my chin and looked him full in the face. "I'm challenging you to a battle, Cameron Dupre."

For the first time since I met him, Cameron's face went slack with shock. "What the fuck did you just say?"

"MR. MANNING." WHITTAKER leaned forward and fold-ed his arms on the table. "In all my time here, I've never had so much controversy surrounding one student."

I wondered if Mr. Dawson was thinking the same thing. He certainly didn't look happy when I said we had to go to the principal's office again.

"No controversy, Mr. Whittaker. All I've done is challenge Cameron to a battle."

"Mr. Dupre is a year ahead of him," said Cameron's teacher, Mrs. Clancy. "It is not allowed as I have told him multiple times, but he insisted that we speak to you because you will agree with him."

Whittaker crooked a brow. "I will, will I? And what makes you believe that, Manning?"

"Because of the rules, sir. Upperclassmen can't challenge younger students, but it doesn't say anything about the other way around."

"That is correct, but only for the fact that it doesn't need to be said. It's foolhardy to challenge someone with more skills and education, and Mr. Dupre here, is at the top of his class."

His words didn't sway me. "It may be foolhardy, but only I will suffer the consequences if I lose."

"Not just you," Cameron snapped. "We have finals next week and I don't have one minute to waste on you, let alone a whole hour for a battle you're going to lose. Forget it."

"Then I'll make it worth your while, Cameron. If I lose, I'll drop out of Breakbattle Academy," I announced. "You won't see me back in here this spring, but on the way out, I'll give you your public apology."

I was on a roll. For the second time in two days, Cameron looked at me in openmouthed shock. Before I could blink, he shot up to Whittaker's desk. "I accept the challenge."

"Hold on!"

"Just a minute!"

Dawson and Clancy shouted at the same time.

"We are the ones who approve challenges," Clancy said. "And I will not grant this. It's nonsense. Zeke has chosen math, but he is in Algebra I which is way below Cameron's level. Cameron is also captain of the basketball team. Sir, I'm sure you can see where this is going. I cannot in good conscience allow this student to give up his place at the academy because he has not thought this through."

"I have thought this through," I protest. "I've had basketball practice almost every day and there is no reason we have to do an Algebra I test. I've gotten into the Archimedean Club. I've proved I can handle advanced mathematics and Mrs. Peterson will say so. We can do the test at Cameron's level so that we *both* have to put in the effort to win."

"Sir, are you hearing this?" Clancy cried. "This is not how we do things."

Whittaker gave no indication that he heard as he stared at me. "Why are you doing this, Mr. Manning?"

"Because Breakbattle is all about pushing past your limits and bucking people's expectations of you, and I finally get that now. We get put into these classes, but it is up to us if we stay there. I can accept that I'm an F, or I can prove that I'm more."

Whittaker's smile didn't tell me what it should. He was unique in that way. He was the only person I ever met who could display an emotion and yet give nothing away. "Well said, Mr. Manning. I'm pleased to see you're finally embracing the spirit of Breakbattle."

"I am, sir. I can face whatever happens."

"Zeke." Dawson moved to my side. "That was a nice speech, but I'm united with Mrs. Clancy on this. I won't approve it either."

"But I will." Whittaker got to his feet. "The battle will go ahead under Mr. Manning's terms. A math test at Dupre's level and the cost of losing is his withdrawal from this school. What will the physical test be?"

"Basketball."

"And what do you want if you win, Manning?"

I flashed Cameron a smile. "I want his chair."

Chapter Six

I walked out of Whittaker's office. Adam leaned against the opposite wall. "How'd it go?"

"He agreed to everything."

Adam's grin no doubt matched mine. "Step three."

"I thought it would be harder than this," I said as we strode off.

The two of us headed back to our room. I slowed down when we walked into our hall and found someone leaning against our door.

Derek sprang up as soon as he saw me. "Manning! What do you think you're doing? You challenged Cameron."

"I had to. It was the only way to end this."

Derek accelerated on me, eyes blazing. "You're not going to end this. You're going to lose and get kicked out of school."

"Thanks for the vote of confidence," I returned. "How did you know about this anyway?"

Adam moved around him. "I'm going to let you guys talk this out. Melody asked me to call her and tell her what happened."

"Cameron texted Santi after Whittaker said yes," Derek replied. "It's all they're talking about upstairs. The deluded little F who thinks he's going to beat the guy who got the highest placement score in his year."

I shrugged. "Good. Let them keep underestimating me."

A groan ripped from his throat. "He's not underestimating you! Cameron is estimating you just fine. He called that you suck at history and you've been losing to his minions all semester. What made you think you can face him and walk away?!"

"Because I've been learning from you."

"He— You— Are you even taking this seriously?!" Derek's face and tone said nothing but anger, but in his eyes, I picked up something else.

"You don't have to worry about me."

"I'm not worried," he snapped.

"I'm doing this for everyone," I continued. "I made a joke about wanting his chair, but what Cameron will actually do when I win is back off me and Cole, Michael, and Landon."

"*When* you win?"

"If I don't win, I'll go to Chesterfield High like I planned."

He shoved away from me, spinning around.

"I had to do something," I said to his back. "He's been getting in the way of what I came here to do. He's gotten me thrown in F Class, forced me to take on more tests and sports, and made me lose friends. It has to stop one way or another."

Derek didn't turn around. He was so still, I wasn't sure he heard me, then came his whispered reply.

"You're just going to leave?"

The question struck me like tiny daggers. I didn't want to leave. I came here for him and there was still more I needed to do.

"No," I said. "I'm just going to win."

THE DAY OF THE BATTLE dawned bright and early. Very early. I woke with the sun to join Michael on the track. Everything had been arranged quickly with Whittaker at the helm. At five o'clock, Cameron and I would battle it out for either the end of my torment or my place at this school. Worry plagued me, rattling my confidence, and running felt like the only thing to do.

Our routine was simple by now. He'd start off lapping the track at a speed I would never be able to run even if I trained all day every day for the rest of my life. Then, Michael would slow and keep pace with me.

I thought today would be different. I braced myself for questions about Cameron and the battle.

None came.

Michael jogged in silence, a soothing presence at my side. Our run was calm. Relaxed.

Perfect.

"THEY SHOULD BE BACK in five minutes," said Mr. Dawson.

I nodded.

"I hope you know what you're doing, Zeke."

"I'm doing what I have to do."

The two of us were alone in Cameron's classroom. The two hadn't been here when we showed up, so we let ourselves in to wait. A few minutes later, the door opened.

"Ah. You're here." Clancy came in and held the door for the people behind her. "Since Mrs. Peterson is being considered his math teacher in this case, we crafted the test together. She has asked to sit in."

"That's no problem," said Dawson.

Peterson walked in, then Cameron. He smiled at me as he walked to his desk—that heart-stopping, radiant smile that bowled me over the first time we met.

I stared blankly at him. You couldn't be fooled by an angel mask when you knew what was underneath.

"Cameron. Zeke. Listen closely," Clancy began. "You will have thirty minutes to complete this test and no more. There are a total of fifteen equations."

She placed a single sheet of paper on my desk.

"You may begin."

I flipped over the paper and read the first question. The room was soundless as we worked. No one coughed. No one sneezed. The clock did not voice its ticks. Or it may have seemed that way as I blocked out all but the numbers.

I didn't think of Cameron or how he was doing. I did not worry about what was at stake. I just did what I was good at: the math.

"Time."

I set down my pencil and pushed back from the desk.

"Mrs. Peterson will stay back and grade your tests," said Dawson. "Follow us. Coach Singh is waiting."

The four of us left the classroom and discovered people waiting for us. Adam, Cole, Michael, Landon, and Derek stood in the hallway.

Derek looked away when I met his eyes.

He had been acting strangely for a while now. He stopped eating with us and barely spoke to me since he found out about the battle against Cameron.

At least he's here, I thought, willing my heart not to sink.

As a quiet group, we left the main building and crossed the lawn for the stadium. Coach Singh rose from the bench when we stepped in.

"Gentlemen, this will be the most interesting battle we've ever held or"—he cut eyes to me—"the saddest," he finished.

The bleachers had been fixed, but the Elite boys took seats on the floor instead of testing it. I got the hint. They were watching this play out.

"The rules are simple," Singh continued. "Thirty minutes on the clock. The one with the most points on the board when it sounds is the winner."

"Yes."

"I'm ready," I said.

"On the court."

Cameron and I faced off, eyes connecting over the ball. I could read his confidence in his eyes, but who knew what he saw in mine.

Fweet!

The ball soared above our heads and as one we leaped, fingers straining for the prize.

Cameron knocked it out of my reach and the game began.

It was brutal. Cameron played hard and he played to win. He was on me relentlessly. Behind my back and then in front of me when I turned around. Breathing down my neck as I dribbled. Smacking my hands when I tried to make a shot. Through it all, Derek's coaching played on a loop in my mind.

"Dribble with your head up. Don't bounce too hard. Stay in control. Eyes open. Use your fingertips. Bend your legs."

Cameron slipped the ball out from under me and took off down the court. He sank another shot while I was wheezing at the center line. Then he sank another one by the time I finally reached him.

He evaded me, playing with me, as I got stuck at his back.

"It's life," Derek whispered to me. *You practice the best you can and then you get out here, everything goes to shit, and from there, instinct takes over."*

I ducked under him and slapped the ball out of his hands. Moving faster than I ever had in my life, I chased it down, and then ran it to the other side of the court. Cameron's shoes smacked on the polished court as he chased me.

I skidded to a stop, lifted my hands, and let go just as he caught up to me. Cameron's hand swiped empty air as the ball sailed out of his reach.

Time slowed as the ball hit and bounced on the metal. It swirled around the rim, teasing me, before tipping forward and sinking through the hoop.

Buzz!

The buzzer rivaled the sound of Cameron's laughter. He snatched up the ball and stuck it under his arm as he turned on me.

"What were you thinking, Manning? You couldn't have thought this would go any other way."

My gaze drifted over his head to the scoreboard. The one that said I lost by six points.

"Manning. Dupre," Coach Singh called. "Get over here."

Coach was standing by the door surrounded by Dawson, Clancy, and Mrs. Peterson.

Peterson stepped forward. "The principal asked that the scores be calculated as soon as possible. He's just as interested in the outcome."

Cameron tossed a grin over his shoulder as he jogged up to them. "I won," he stated. "I didn't get any of the math questions wrong and I beat him by six points. It's over."

I saw the Elite boys share a look.

"I'll hold up my end," I rasped. "I won't be back after winter break."

Peterson shook her head. "I'm sorry, Zeke."

"It's okay. I did my best."

"But you are mistaken. You will not be leaving the academy."

I froze. What did she just say?

"What?!"

"Zeke Manning has won the battle."

"But that's not possible," Cameron cried. "I didn't get the problems wrong. I know I didn't!"

Peterson kept her voice even. "Yes, you are right in that every question you answered was correct, but you did not answer every question. You only answered fourteen."

"I ran out of time!"

"But Zeke did not. He answered every problem correctly for a score of a hundred. You I could give no more than ninety-three."

The ball went flying as Cameron swung out his arm, gesturing at the court. "But we both got an A and I won the game."

Coach Singh shook his head. "Academic tests are weighted more. He would have needed to lose to you by eight points or more for you to make up the difference. He won, Cameron. A homeschooled freshman from the F Class beat the junior varsity basketball captain." Singh gave him a hard look. "You and I are going to have a talk about your probation tomorrow. Hit the showers."

"But, Coach!"

Singh stalked out of the stadium.

"Coach!" Cameron knocked me out of the way to run after him.

Clancy and Peterson followed him albeit at a slower pace.

"Well done, Zeke," Dawson said. "I'm glad I won't be losing my favorite student."

I fought a smile. "I don't think you're allowed to have favorites, sir."

He winked. Only when the door closed behind him did I turn around. The guys were all on their feet, staring at me. One broke from the pack.

Adam took a step toward me and looked me square in the eyes.

"Whoooo!"

I busted out laughing. Adam threw his head back, shouting at the top of his lungs, and the others were right behind him.

I had enough time for my eyes to get big before they were on me. They hoisted me in the air, whooping and cheering.

Eventually, they set me down and we took the party back to Landon's dorm.

"I'll be happy if I never do a damn battle again," said Landon. He tossed himself on his bed. "I'm taking full advantage of this 'choosing your champion' thing from now on and passing every challenge to Cole."

Cole shot him his patented scowl. "Why me?"

Landon shrugged. "'Cause I don't like you very much."

"Screw you."

I rolled my eyes. They weren't any closer to being friends with each other, but at least they were friends with me.

Something moved out of the corner of my eye. Derek moved the armchair closer to the window, and farther from everyone else.

"Hey," I said as I drew near him. "Are we okay?"

He kept his eyes fixed on the view. "Why wouldn't we be?"

"You've been kind of weird lately. Weirder than usual."

"No, I haven't."

I sat down on the arm of the chair. "You haven't eaten with us in a while and you've been quiet the last few days. I miss us hanging out."

"You miss us hanging out?" He twisted his neck to give me a look. "We don't have to hang out every day, Zeke. Wow. You're worse than a girlfriend."

"I am worse than a girlfriend." I bumped his shoulder. "I'm a friend."

"I don't know why you think we're friends."

Humming, I rolled my eyes up to the ceiling. "Maybe it's because... you came to watch the battle because you were worried about me."

"I wasn't worried!"

"You were totally worried. You would have missed me so much if I didn't come back."

Derek put his hand on my thigh and tried to shove me off. Thinking fast, I grabbed his arm. Derek jerked back and the next thing I knew I was looking up from his lap. We took one look at each other and laughed so hard my sides split.

"I'm glad I'm staying," I said when I caught my breath. "This place is crazy, but I belong here."

"No one is going to question that after today."

He smiled and I smiled back...

...until he bucked and dumped me on the floor.

All the boys laughed themselves sick, Derek loudest of all. After a beat, I did too.

Everything was back to how it was supposed to be.

"ZELA? HEY, ZEE!"

I poked my head out of the kitchen. "What is it?"

"Hurry up so you can tell me about your master plan. How did you pull it off?"

"One sec." I took the popcorn out of the microwave and dumped it into a bowl. Jordan was spread out on the couch when I came back in, remote in hand. "You said I could pick the movie."

"I lied."

Laughing, I pushed her feet aside and sat down. Winter break had officially arrived. I survived finals week and practically ran to Mom's car after the last bell rang. I itched to be Zela again.

"Just for that, I won't tell you how you gave me the idea that turned everything around."

"Ooh. Now, you have to tell me." She sat up and rested her chin on her knees. "How did I save the day?"

"I realized the key to making it stop had to do with something I've always said: everything is math."

"How does math figure into getting back at that Cameron guy?"

"It's simple. The first step was getting Derek and the boys to help train me. A bunch of angry guys pissed at being used, plus a chance to get him back, equals help on my sports game.

"Step two was getting into the Archimedean Club. When you suggested Orlov was picking hard questions because he could, I thought how much easier it would be if Dawson chose the question. He'd never mess with me by giving me a test on something he didn't teach me. That's why I challenged the B guy, Miles, to a history test. Dawson chose and our test was on the Trail of Tears. I won and got into the club."

I snuggled into the cushions and grabbed a handful of popcorn. "Getting into the club was leverage that led to step three. Add one principal who sees us as guinea pigs, an arrogant alpha held back from striking directly against me, and an offer he couldn't refuse. All of that equaled a final battle to put an end to it once and for all."

I grinned at her as I shoved the treat in my mouth. "You see?" I mumbled. "Math."

"Not bad, Zee. Not bad at all." She leaned back. "There's only one thing. Do you think Cameron will hold up his end of the deal?"

"I hope so. I'm done with drama. I literally got dragged into all of that Network stuff and it went horribly wrong. I just want to get back on track."

She held up an imaginary glass. "To getting back on track."

I followed suit. "Getting back on track. From now on, it's all about Derek."

WINTER BREAK WAS SO wonderful, I didn't want it to end. Mom and Aunt Bev surprised us with another trip to New York City. We ice-skated, walked among the Christmas lights, and ran through a department store with permission to grab anything we wanted as a Christmas gift.

Waking up that morning to go back to Breakbattle was tough, especially because Jordan had one more week off while I had to return to school.

"Zela, are you packed?"

I swallowed my mouthful of oatmeal before answering. "Yes, I put my bags in the car already."

"Good," she said, somewhat distractedly. Her laptop was sitting next to her breakfast and only one of them was getting her attention. "So what will you do about the organization?"

"What organization?"

"Stand Up." Mom pointed at her screen. "I'm editing the chapter on civic engagement, and I included Breakbattle's response to your protest." She peered at me over her glasses. "I'm assuming you're not giving up."

There was only one right answer to that. "No, Mom. We're not giving up. It's been harder because our club activities are strictly monitored. They triple-check every poster we make and boys and girls aren't allowed to cross campuses, so meeting up in secret is hard. But Melody is nothing if not determined."

Mom hummed. "I'm glad to hear it. When you return, I want you to ask Melody if she'll consider being interviewed for the book. I'll get her parents' permission too of course."

"I'll ask her, but you won't accidentally mention your daughter if she interviews you back?" I teased.

She laughed. "I will be very careful, but the truth is, I've been enjoying having a son." She got up from the table and pressed a kiss to my forehead. "We have so much more to talk about."

"Like how boys' bathrooms don't have pad dispensers when you need them and their pants bunch up weird around your hips."

"Exactly." She kissed me again. "You're learning the plight of a woman by posing as a man. You're getting the education my book intends to impart. Now, finish that and let's go."

The trip to Breakbattle was quick, and an hour and a half later, I walked into my tiny dorm and found Adam had already arrived. Mom said her goodbyes and we went off to round up our friends and spend our last free day messing around. The next morning, we woke early to grab breakfast.

"Why do you think we're having an assembly?" I asked Adam.

"Mom said there're going to be some changes."

"Good changes?"

"She didn't say, so I'm guessing not."

Unease settled in my gut and made my favorite breakfast look unappealing. I took my French toast to our usual table, worrying my lip all the way. Were these changes to the battle system? Were they announcing our organs were up for grabs now too? Or were they cracking down on student organizations? Or maybe they knew who sabotaged the Elite seats?

"What are you stressing about now?"

I blinked back to reality. "What?"

"You've got that look," Owen continued. "What is it?"

"The assembly. Just wondering if it's going to be good or bad for us."

"I say good," a voice said. I jerked my head up as Derek sat down on my side. "Whittaker shook things up with his random changes to the system, and Dad went on about it all break. I bet some of the parents called him on it and now he's getting things back to normal."

I barely heard a word he said. "Derek, you're here."

He was here. He was sitting with me. Was the weirdness between us over and we were back to being friends?

"Of course, I'm here. Where else would I be? I go to school here, dumbass."

Hard to say. He blesses his enemies and his friends with his winning personality.

"How was your break?" I asked.

He shrugged as he sliced up his French toast. "Decent. We went to Switzerland and didn't get back until late last night. I'm running on jetlag and espressos. You?"

"We went to the city again. It was amazing."

"You and your cousin/girlfriend?"

"You know I don't like you, right?"

Derek laughed. For the first time since he sat down, he faced me fully and smiled into my eyes. "Liar."

"Hey, guys."

The greeting made me break eye contact. We all said hi to Melody as she sat down. Derek just grunted.

"Melody," I spoke up. "My mom is writing a book about female empowerment, and she wanted to know if you'd like to be interviewed."

She blinked. "Me? Why me?"

"I told her about you and she's impressed with all you've done to push back against the system. The offer might come to replace me, but please don't take it, I won't do well on the streets."

She giggled. "Don't worry. I haven't decided to trade in my parents just yet. Tell her I'll do it for sure. It's so cool she even thought of me."

"How was your break, Melody?" Adam asked.

She lost her smile. "Not great. Cameron and I broke up."

"What?" I froze with my fork halfway to my mouth. "You did?"

She nodded. "He was raging after he lost to you in that battle. He was saying crazy things, like how I knew what you were planning to do, and I was on your side the whole time. When I asked what did it matter if he won or lost when we thought the whole system was stupid anyway, he flipped. The conversation got... hurtful, so I ended it."

"I'm sorry, Melody." My heart ached for her. Cameron deserved to be dumped and hard, but I never wanted her to get hurt in the process. At least I was right about one thing, he hadn't been able to hide his true self for long.

"You deserve better." My mouth fell open as Adam reached across the table and took her hand. "I'm sorry."

She smiled softly. "Thanks, Adam." I barely held back a squeal when she rested her other hand on top of theirs.

"That's happening if it hasn't already." Derek's breath ghosted over my ear. "And I thought Moon didn't know how to play."

"This isn't a game," I whispered back. "It's love."

He snorted, but didn't say any more.

"Students." The call drew our attention to the head table. "Finish your breakfast and begin heading to the auditorium," said Argyle. "We wish to start on time so you don't miss too much of the school day."

I dug into my French toast and ate quickly. Soon we were dumping our trash and making the walk to the auditorium. There was a full stage once again. All the teachers and staff were present which added weight to the feeling that this was important.

"Come in, come in," Argyle called. "Fill the front rows first."

Adam, Justin, Owen, Derek, and I claimed spots in the third row. We traded guesses on what this could be about as we waited for it to begin.

"Is everyone here?" she asked. "Close the doors."

"No. Everyone is not here." Orlov rose from his seat. "The Elite students are missing."

"Missing?"

Dozens of heads swung this way and that, looking for the telltale E. Besides Derek, I couldn't see Landon, Michael, or Cole anywhere.

Argyle sighed. "Will someone find them, please? Check the dorm and the cafeteria."

"I'll go." Orlov stepped off the stage and hurried to find his tardy favorites.

"We'll begin as soon as everyone is present," Argyle assured us.

I shifted toward Derek as we settled in to wait. "Tell me more about Switzerland. What did you guys do?"

"Visited family, hiked, and rode trains."

"Wow," I said when he finished. "You have to stop with the long, drawn-out stories. I fell asleep in the middle there."

He chuckled. "There's not much to tell. It was pretty boring."

"Did you go to Interlaken? Mom and I loved it there. We paraglided off a mountain."

"You've been paragliding too?" He sounded the tiniest bit impressed. "Let me guess, your pictures are on your other phone."

"Yeah. What about you? Where are your pictures?"

I perked up as he pulled out his cell. "Not much to see though."

"Which part of your family lives in Switzerland?" I pored over his photos as he swiped.

"My dad's parents. He put them up in style when he made his first million."

Derek stopped on the photo of a sweet elderly couple. I slipped the phone from his grasp for a better look.

"What are their na—?"

Bang!

"Mrs. Argyle! Principal Whittaker!"

Dozens of heads snapped around as Orlov burst into the room.

"What on earth is going on?" Argyle cried.

Orlov raced up the stairs. We couldn't hear what he said to her, but his hands waved wildly. Suddenly, Argyle shot away and grabbed the microphone. "Students, you're dismissed!"

That was all she said before she spun around, beckoned the other staff, and they all raced through the back of the stage.

"Damn," Adam whispered. "What happened?"

"YOU WANT TO KNOW WHAT happened?" Nico said as he dumped his books on the desk. "The Elite students were trapped in their rooms."

"Trapped?!" Adam, Tanner, and I cried at the same time.

"How?" Tanner added.

"Someone messed with the locks from the outside. All the Elites, freshmen to seniors, were shouting their heads off, banging on the door to get out when Orlov found them. Only Derek was spared because he never went to his room, but his lock was messed with too."

I gaped at Nico, trying to make sense of what he was saying. "How do you know this?"

"One of the custodians told me."

"Why did they tell you?"

"Because she's my cousin." Nico pulled out his phone. "She also sent me this."

The three of us almost bumped heads leaning in to see. On his screen was a picture of a door and—

I squinted. *What is that?*

"An upside-down A," Nico announced. "Whoever did it stuck it on all the doors."

"Why?" I asked. "What's the point of that?"

"Marking their prank."

Tanner straightened. "Another prank? Like the basketball bleachers?"

"But that wasn't funny," said Adam. "Someone could have gotten hurt. Being locked in with your television, computer, and bathroom is harmless compared to that."

I nodded. "That's true. Also, it was just the guys because Melody wasn't locked in her room. Do you think it was someone else?"

"I would if it wasn't for..." Adam trailed off as he gazed at the upturned A.

What did it mean that this was on the door and our posters?

"Word gets around fast."

We jumped. I even let out a yelp.

Mr. Dawson bent down and took the phone from Nico. "I will not ask how you got this," he said softly, "but I will tell you the principal wants this to be kept quiet while they investigate who is behind these pranks. He is livid and the punishment he's planning is on the wrong side of harsh. Do not give anyone reason to think it's you by having photos you shouldn't have."

"Yes, Mr. Dawson," Nico mumbled.

He handed it back. "Delete this, please."

Nico did so while Dawson walked up to the front to start class. I kept my promise not to talk about it for no more than a few hours.

"Did you guys see or hear anything?"

Landon pulled his helmet on and secured it. "Nothing. I woke up, got dressed, turned the knob, and realized I wasn't going anywhere."

"This is so strange. Do you think it has to do with the bleachers?"

Sighing, he climbed off the bench and strode over to the mat. "I don't think anything except that it better not happen again," he said as he got into position. "Whittaker and Argyle say they'll handle it. There's a match coming up and I need to focus. Let's go, Manning. We're doing lifts today."

I bit back a groan. Landon may have looked pretty, but he was a beast on the mat and he didn't tolerate complaining. He was extra dispassionate with me since I asked him to teach me, not the other way around.

I faced off with him and got into the stance he taught me. "Just don't throw me around, okay?"

He grinned. "I won't. Takedowns are all about control. Throwing and slamming is illegal."

"It didn't seem illegal last week," I muttered.

"What was that?"

"Nothing."

Landon called it and practice started. I actually learned a lot from him. He narrated as he took me down and pinned me, and then at the end, he let me try it on him.

"Okay, so I... grab your waist and secure your hands," I whispered as I pulled him to me. "Lower my hips. Is this right?"

Landon twisted around and his cheek brushed my forehead. "A little more."

I bent my legs. "Alright, then I hold tight, push with my legs, thrust my hips forward and—" I grunted under Landon's full weight. Moving quickly, but carefully, I brought him down to the mat. "That's it," I breathed. I looked around like I couldn't believe how I got here. "I did it!"

"Not bad." Landon grinned up at me, his gold eyes glinting with mirth. "I thought I'd be too heavy, but you're not so scrawny after all."

I tried to laugh with him. My breath came in short spurts, half the pace they should be, while my heart beat so fast he might have felt it if my bindings weren't between us. My eyes traced his face, traveling over his flawless skin and lingering on his full lips. All it would take to capture those lips was to bend my neck.

"Ah, Manning?" Landon scrunched up his face. "You can let me up now."

"Oh! Sorry." I scrambled off him. My face burned so hot; I ducked my head rather than let him see I was red.

"My turn." Two hands grabbed me and spun me around. Landon pulled me flush against his body. "You ready?"

I fought not to smile. "I'm ready."

THE SECOND SEMESTER was a mess of games, events, and competitions, and most of the school was consumed by it. Sports mattered just as much as academics at Breakbattle. The fever struck everyone and it was only the first week back. The next day, Adam woke early to hit the pool while I went out to run with Michael.

"When is your first meet?" I huffed. Michael didn't like a lot of talking when we ran, but I figured I could entice him with his favorite subject.

"Next month. First week of March. In through the nose, Manning. It's all about your breathing."

I matched my breathing the way he taught me. "Adam's swim meet is before that. Then there's Landon's wrestling match. Also, my cousin said Chesterfield and Breakbattle are doing a rematch, but they want it to be on their court."

There was going to be a rematch and Derek was going to play. Cameron would too, but as co-captain of the team. Coach Singh hadn't taken it away from him completely, but that demotion had to sting.

"I heard that too. Can't blame them," he said. "One more lap and then we'll call it. I have to meet up with Cole to study."

"Study for what? It's the second day."

He chuckled. "That means nothing to Orlov. He's testing us to make sure we didn't forget everything over the break."

We ran one more lap, and then jogged over to the benches. Michael picked up his water bottle while I got off my feet.

"Where's your water?"

I shook my head. "Forgot it."

"Have some of mine."

"No, it's fine. I—"

"Drink, Manning." He grabbed my hand and wrapped my fingers around the bottle. "You have to stay hydrated."

The bottle shook a little as I brought it to my lips. I knew I was being weird, but I could not put aside the fact that Michael had put his lips on this.

He put it away after I took my tentative sip and gathered his things. "See you later."

I hopped off the bench. "I'll come with. Adam will be there too."

Michael and I had perfect timing. We walked in just as Nelson ordered the boys out of the water. "Great work today, guys. Get cleaned up."

Adam and Cole went in to change and came out twenty minutes later walking side by side. Cole was showing him something on his phone.

What's going on with this?

Last I knew, Cole couldn't stand Adam, and Adam was amused by his extreme competitiveness.

"What's up?" I asked.

Adam's hair was still damp from his shower. Water swirled the length of his curls and dripped onto his shoulder. "Admin sent out announcements about the assembly. Derek was right about the changes to the system."

Michael took the phone from Cole. "What kind of changes?"

"Things are going back the way they were. They made a list of what you can have battles over and personal items aren't on it." Adam threw me a look. "And you can only challenge people in your grade."

"I guess I'm not surprised," I said as we set off for the dorm. "Anything else?"

"It said they are handing out new handbooks today," said Cole, "because they made updates to the definition of bullying and the consequences."

We didn't need to ask what brought that on. The four of us split in the main hallway. Cole and Michael went to study, and Adam and I went back to our dorm.

I quickly got in the shower before the alarms went off and was out as the other boys were shuffling to the bathroom. In class, Dawson confirmed everything Cole told us. The battle system was going back to the way it was and bullies, pranksters, and damage to school property would result in suspension or expulsion.

Maybe the person responsible got the hint because we got to Friday with no more incidents—against the Elites anyway.

A hard shove almost propelled me into the tray stack. "Ow! Watch where you're going?!"

Zach sneered. "You watch where you're going. You cut Shannon off. How fucking rude is that?"

A pretty brunette, Shannon most likely, claimed my spot in line as Zach passed her a tray. He grinned like a smug fool when she kissed his cheek.

My grip tightened on the tray. There was the tiniest part of me that wanted to smack him across the face with it. Zach had been an annoyance all week. Bumping into me, making nasty comments whenever I walked by, yukking it up with his friends at the Elite table and pointing me out, so I knew they were talking about me. He was being awful, but to my surprise...

I glanced across the table at the sophomore Elites.

Cameron and his buddies hadn't said a word to me. None of them so much as looked in my direction and according to Cole, Michael, and Derek, they hadn't said anything to them either. Cameron was keeping up his side of the deal.

Shifting narrowed eyes to Zach, I struggled to keep my anger down. *Cameron may be over it, but this thing between me and Zach is personal.*

He turned his back on me as Adam came up. "Hey. Everything cool?"

"I'm fine."

"Zeke, before I forget, do you want to stay at my place this weekend? Mom had the baby."

"Aww. I wish I could, but I'm staying on campus. Mom is going to a conference. She shuts her phone off during these things, so I can't call and ask her to let me out. I'm going to be a weekender for the first time."

I thanked the server and we headed back to our table.

"That's too bad. You can come over another time."

"Okay," I said, but I really wanted to go.

I rang Mom all day between classes, and finally gave Aunt Bev a call.

"What is it, Zee?"

"Do you have the number for Mom's hotel?" I peeked through the gap in the bathroom stall. I was less than comfortable being in the boys' bathroom even after all this time, but I didn't want my phone taken away. "I want to stay at Adam's house this weekend."

"You don't need your mom. She told the school I have permission to sign you out." Her voice turned sharp. "But explain to me why you need to stay over at a boy's house?"

"Adam isn't a boy. He's... Adam! He's my friend. He thinks I'm a guy, and he's in love with someone who is not me. I just want to meet his new sister. That's it."

She hummed. "Well, I guess I can trust your school therapist to look out for you. Have you told her the truth yet?"

I stiffened against the plastic. "There isn't anything to tell."

"I meant about you being a girl. She has to keep those things secret."

"I don't think breaking school rules falls under that, Auntie. I can't say anything, but I can meet her baby. Please, please, please."

"Alright, alright. I'll call the school now."

"Thank you!" I gushed. "I love you. You're my favorite aunt."

"That means so much considering I'm your only aunt," she said with a hint of tease. "I love you too. Talk to you later."

I rushed out of the bathroom, threw some things in a bag, and caught up to Adam in front of the school gates. His driver whisked us out of Breakbattle to their full mansion, made even fuller by the newest member of the family, Jessica Van Zandt.

"That is a great name," I said as Adam put the baby in my arms. We were in one of the living rooms with a movie on pause and about a dozen snacks on the coffee table when Adam left and returned with Jessica. "Where is your mom?"

"She and Jaxson are passed out on the bed." He plopped down next to me. "Jessie was awake so I took her."

"Is that okay?"

He laughed. "Yeah. We're good. She'd rather hang out with us anyway."

The baby let out a soft grunt as if she were agreeing with her brother. A smile spread across my lips as I looked down at her. She was impossibly tiny while having the biggest, most beautiful blue eyes I had ever seen. Wisps of delicate blonde hair peeked through her cap and she stared at me as I adjusted it.

"She is so beautiful," I whispered.

"You think so?" Adam peered over my shoulder. "I think she looks like a wet sponge."

I made a choked noise. "Adam!"

"What?" he said between chuckles. "Babies are never cute when they first come out. Give her a few months and she'll be the most adorable thing around here."

"She already is," I said firmly. "Ugh. Boys."

Adam nudged me. "You're a boy too."

"But I'm a boy that knows how beautiful you are," I cooed at her. "Such a pretty baby."

Laughing, Adam flicked the movie on again and we settled in to watch. Twenty minutes in, Jessie fell asleep and the sweet, peaceful look on her little face threatened to make my heart burst. I loved babies, but rarely got the chance to be around them. I envied Adam for getting to grow up with so many siblings   even Esme.

"Adam? Adam?"

"We're in here, Mom," he called.

"Do you have Jessie?"

"No, Zeke does."

Val appeared in the entryway. It was strange seeing her outside of our sessions. She was neutral and business-casual in that space, but this was home. She glided across the room in a simple dress, the picture of relaxed and happy.

"Did she wake up?" she asked.

"Yep, but we got her back down."

Val glanced at the screen. "To a violent action-thriller."

"Just a little brother-sister bonding, Mom."

She laughed. "I see. Well, thank you for watching her. Jaxson and I needed the nap but"—Val gave me a knowing look—"may I have my daughter now?"

I grimaced. "I'm trying, but it's so hard to let her go."

"I know exactly how you feel." She bent and gently gathered the sleeping baby in her arms. "Dinner will be in a little bit, boys, so don't fill up on those snacks."

Of course, we didn't listen, but dinner was delicious anyway. The whole weekend was a mix of movies, games, food, and hanging out with the whole family. So unlike the life I had growing up, but a gift to be a part of.

Monday came too quickly. The second week, and school was getting back to normal.

Mrs. Peterson was her usual happy self when she welcomed us inside.

"Another semester of Archimedean Club, but I say this will be the most interesting one yet," she said. "We've trained. We've sharpened our minds. We've done so many relays that I've been seeing numbers in my sleep. We are ready for the competition."

I raised my hand.

"Yes, Zeke?"

"How does it work? Do we all compete?"

"No, Only four members can represent a school. From those who are interested, we'll select our best." She moved over to her desk. "I have photos from our previous competitions to tempt— I mean, show you. Then if you're interested, you'll write a short speech on why you should be chosen, and then we'll have a silent vote."

She woke up her computer. "First, there is the county competition." A picture of three members and Santi appeared on the smartboard. He looked seconds away from a nap. Actually, he could have been napping—who knew. "County is against the Chesterfield team.

"Last year, Santiago brought us the victory and we went on to the state competition. It was great fun. We stayed at a hotel, explored the town, and went out to dinner with the other teams." She tapped her keyboard. "This is us at—"

The screen went black.

"Oh. What happened? I must have pressed the wrong button." Mrs. Peterson bent over, squinting at the computer. "I'm still getting the hang of this smartboard. Very temperamental."

"Mrs. Peterson? What is that?"

Her eyes grew huge. "I... don't know."

Murmurs broke out around me as something appeared on the screen. It wasn't a photo of a bunch of math enthusiasts smiling over pasta.

"Zeke," Cole whispered. "That looks like the—"

"An upside-down A."

"WE CAN SAY FOR SURE now that something is going on," I said.

Cole shoved aside his food. "But what? Are we supposed to understand this?"

Our table was full for dinner that night. Cole and Michael always sat by themselves, but he had stuck to me since I told him I saw the same A on our posters the day of the basketball game. He passed it on to Michael, who mentioned it to Landon, and Derek overheard them. Friends or not, here they were.

"It doesn't make sense," Michael added. "The bleachers, the dorms, the computers. They're coming after the Elite for sure, but why?"

"He must have a reason," said Melody. "That creepy A appeared on our computers too. When we left, the IT guy was still working on getting rid of it. He said it was some kind of virus."

"He?" Derek questioned.

She nodded. "It has to be a boy."

Everyone exchanged looks, except for me. "She's right. It does. That's why the girls weren't locked in their dorms. It's a guy and they knew getting caught walking around the girls' campus would be a disaster. They couldn't risk it."

Adam inclined his head. "Makes sense, but who? Who did you guys piss off?"

"We're not the only Elites," Michael said. "Someone might have a problem with the seniors and they're taking it out on all of us."

"That's true," I muttered, mostly to myself. This could be about any or all of them. "But why did they put their stickers on our posters?"

No one had an answer for me.

Owen spoke up. "I want to know when he'll stop. This guy is serious, and he's facing expulsion if Whittaker finds him. How far is he going to take this?"

Silence descended on the table. How far would this go? Was this the end or the beginning of something worse? How could we guess when we didn't know why it was happening?

"Landon." A voice broke through my tumultuous thoughts. "Michael. Cole. What are you doing with them? The Elite are sitting over there."

Cole's lip curled. "What did you say? It's never been your business where the fuck I sit, Fields, and it's not today either."

"Really? You're friends with Manning after everything? He's not one of us."

I didn't turn around as his shadow cast over my spot. "Zach, give it a rest," I said calmly. "I'm not interested in a war with you. I never was. Even Cameron has gone back to his own life, why can't you do the same?"

"What did you just say?" A hand clamped painfully on my shoulder.

"Ah!"

Screech!

Derek's chair shrieked along the floor and toppled over. He moved only a hair faster than Adam and Owen. Zach's hand disappeared as he stumbled back.

"I'm a peaceful guy," Derek hissed, "but you're getting on my nerves. Back the fuck off, Zach, or you'll be the next one to get your face bashed in, and I *am* one of you. So consider that a promise, brother."

"Go, Zach." I couldn't see Adam's eyes through the curtain of his hair, but his voice chilled me. "You made your choice."

"Adam, I... did the right thing." Now I turned around. There was no sneer or mocking smile on Zach's face. The shield had come down for the barest moment and his pain laid bare. "It was a trick. Derek was in on it! I was right not to stay for him. I would have lost everything if I fell for his game."

"That wasn't the choice I was talking about."

Slowly, Zach turned to Owen. I felt the seconds pass like physical blows, beating into me as they stared at each other. Owen was the first to look away. He turned his back on his friend and walked out.

Zachary didn't follow. He didn't speak. He just went back to his table.

"What was that about?" Melody asked.

Adam shook his head. "I'm going for a walk. Clear my head. Then, I'll find Owen."

"Want some company?"

It was the barest twitch of the lips, but it was a smile. "I'd love some."

Side by side, the two walked out. They hadn't reached the door before Melody slipped her hand in his.

"You didn't have to do that," I said to Derek.

"Yes, I did." He picked up his fork and stabbed a green bean. "We're friends."

Chapter Seven

Soon, life settled into a routine that was almost normal. If normal could be applied to a place like Breakbattle. The challenges stopped coming since I had no privileges and Cameron went back to ruling over the sophomores. I was free to study for regular classes, wrestle and play soccer with Landon, run with Michael, and go to math club with Cole.

As for the mysterious prankster, the IT people removed the virus, but no one claimed credit or was caught. Since then, weeks passed and things had been quiet. No attacks. No stickers. We put him out of our minds to focus on getting through the year.

I zipped up my suit and headed out of the locker room. Tanner stifled a laugh when he saw me.

"Are you going to do that every time?" I asked.

"Dude, have you seen yourself?"

My cheeks warmed. My swimsuit deserved the looks it got. I knew it. "This was the best I could do," I said. "Better than a zero."

"Is it, though?"

I ignored him and claimed a seat on the edge of the pool with the beginners. Coach Nelson stood in the water, ready for his last block of the day.

"Today, we're continuing practice with the freestyle stroke. You're doing well, but it's important to remember to come up for air, flutter your feet, and swim straight. Tanner, Dustin, and Kim, you're first. Zeke, I want you in that corner practicing treading water."

Groaning, I slipped into the pool and paddled to my spot. I had mastered every lesson Nelson taught me except for this one. He was committed to changing that.

"Coach, is it possible there are people who just can't float?"

"No."

"But I've been trying for weeks and all I do is sink."

Nelson drifted closer to me while keeping one eye on the swimmers. "Everything takes practice, Zeke. Make sure all four limbs are in action. Keep upright and move your legs like you're riding a bicycle."

"Okay, I'll try."

I kicked off the bottom and got all my limbs in gear, kicking and flapping like a loon. My lips dipped below the surface, then Nelson disappeared as I was claimed by the water. I shot up sputtering.

"Keep trying, Manning. Just slow it down. Don't panic."

I spent the entire block in my corner and I wasn't treading water by the end of it. After the other boys left, I went into the locker room, showered, dressed, and came out to find Tanner waiting for me.

"Nico and Adam saved us seats for the match."

"Nice. Let's go."

The trip to the wrestling arena was a short one. The line outside of the arena was not. This was the first big match after the basketball game, and three other schools were here to compete against our junior varsity wrestling team.

We skirted the line and strode in looking for Adam and Nico. No separate seating by class this time. Everyone sat where they wanted while Whittaker and Argyle looked on.

I spotted them in the front row. "I can't wait to see my first real wrestling match," I said as I claimed my seat. "I've earned it after being Landon's practice dummy."

"Was it that bad?"

A vision of Landon pinned under me popped into my head. "No... not that bad."

The room filled up until we could barely hear each other over the roar of the crowd. The thrill of a match surged through the room. It filled me with energy as I bounced on my seat, eager for things to start.

"Welcome, everyone," the announcer began. "It's a pleasure to have all of you here to cheer your students on to victory."

"Yeah!" we whooped.

"Let's not waste any time." The man introduced the judges, and finally, the first pair stepped up to the mat and faced off.

Thanks to Landon, I could follow the match and name the moves. I noticed instantly when the boy from Westfall Prep messed up his takedown. He lost his balance and his opponent got the upper hand. Westfall lost quickly after that.

"Next up is Landon Foster from Breakbattle Academy and Philip North from Timothy MacDonnell High."

Landon emerged from the back and took his place.

"Gentlemen, shake hands."

Timothy stepped forward to shake. Landon paused to rub his eyes before doing the same.

I wonder what color his contacts are and how his opponents don't find it distracting. They were all I could look at when we wrestled.

It's no wonder why you'd get distracted, another voice spoke up as they began to circle each other. *I think most people can keep their heads better than that.*

Timothy dove. He took hold of Landon for a takedown and the boys went down smooth. My dreamy thoughts evaporated as he grabbed his arms. Was Landon about to be pinned in the first ten seconds?

Landon slipped out of his hold and scrambled to his feet. I let out the breath I had been holding. Coach was watching. The whole school was watching. He had to win.

Landon let out a groan as he shook it out.

Good. Get back in the flow.

He squared with Timothy once again. Timothy didn't do the dance. He came in fast, geared up for another takedown.

"Ah! Ahhhh!"

Timothy skidded to a stop inches from Landon, face scrunching up. He hadn't laid a finger on him yet.

Landon's hands flew to his face. He clawed at his eyes, screams growing louder.

The cheers died down—not in an abrupt end, but slow as the time it took my smile to melt away.

"Landon?" I jumped from my seat at the same time Argyle, Whittaker, and the ref ran to him. "Landon!"

THE DOOR OPENED WITH a soft whoosh of air.

"You can come in now, dear."

I stood before she finished her sentence. The nurse held open the door for me to go in.

"You can't stay for long. He needs to rest."

My eyes were fixed on the figure lying within white linens. "Landon?" I called. The blankets stirred. "Are you okay?"

I pulled a chair closer to the bed and sat down. His raven locks splayed out on the pillow, drawing my eyes to the only part of him visible.

"Manning, is that you?"

"It's me. What happened out there?"

"According to the nurse, someone messed with my contact solution."

My gasp couldn't escape my throat, it closed up so tight. "Y-your— Your eyes?"

"My eyes are fine." In a blink, the blanket was gone. "Or they will be."

I hissed. Gone were the pinks, blues, and golds. Landon's true eye color was a warm brown that was almost impossible to see due to the angry, bloodshot tinge.

"Are you sure? That looks painful."

"I'm sure." He tilted his head back and let his eyelids flutter shut. "They washed my eyes out and it feels much better. Just a little sensitive."

"It was the prankster."

My hand was resting on the edge of the mattress. I moved closer to the pinky I saw poking beneath his sheet, but stopped myself when it was millimeters away. My fingers trembled and I didn't want him to feel my shaking when he was keeping it together so well. "He did this to you."

"They found a sticker in the back room. It was him."

I bit my lip hard. "Why?" I croaked when I could trust my-self. "Why would they do this to you?"

"A lot of people are jealous of the Elite. We get everything. Someone could be trying to embarrass us—prove they're better than us."

"Why are you so calm?" I whispered.

"Because if they really wanted to hurt me... they could have put something much worse in there."

"But the match and the—"

"Hey." I stiffened as his hand came out and rested over mine. "Thanks for coming. Henrietta and Declan are out of the country. It's too quiet in here. Nice not to be alone."

Alone.

Landon was always alone. He sat at tables with people he never talked to. He shared a class with boys he didn't like and who did not like him just as much.

Am I his only friend?

"Then I'll stay," I said.

I turned my palm up and closed my hand over his. We stayed like that for a long time, not saying anything.

THE DAYS MARCHED TOWARD the swim meet, but there wasn't the same energetic vibe as before. Landon's parents returned from Europe and took him out of school for a week to see a doctor and, according to his texts, chew him out for not telling them someone was attacking his class. I grew more wor-ried with every text and every day he wasn't here that he would not come back to the academy.

The morning of the meet, my phone went off as I was lacing my sneakers.

"It's Jordan," I said aloud. "She told me to tell you good luck and be careful."

"Tell her thanks."

I typed in Adam's reply. "How are you feeling about the meet? Nervous? Worried? Excited?"

"No. Not for me. Yes," he rattled off. "I'm not Elite, but Cole and Sullivan are. Mom said they're having security check their stuff before they go on. This is serious."

"But is this person targeting events or are they happy to strike anytime anywhere?"

"The bleachers, the computers, the class-wide assembly no-show. The guy obviously wants everyone to see what he's doing. If he wants to unleash public humiliation on Cole and Sullivan, the meet is too good an opportunity to miss."

The truth of that seeped into my bones like dread. Adam was right.

"I'm relieved they're taking this seriously and stepping up security," he continued. "I don't want to see anyone else get hurt. Landon was... too far."

"You be careful too."

He smiled. "I will. Now let's go. Mom and Ryder are coming to see the meet. They should be here soon."

"Are they bringing the baby?"

"Jessie's not ready for Breakbattle yet."

"Can't blame her. I'm not either."

The tense mood lightened for a moment as we laughed. To-gether, we left the dorm and made for the pool. Stepping out of the main building, we stumbled into a line that stretched the length of the quad. As we got closer to the pool, we saw why.

Security checked bags and waved their wands over the hapless students, parents, and staff.

"One at a time, please," said a familiar voice. "Have your bags open."

I slowed down as we approached Cameron and Santiago. Volunteer read clear on their name tags. I wasn't surprised they stepped up to help out. The cafeteria was filled with grim faces. The separation of the classes was more pronounced than ever. The Elite knew they were under attack.

Cameron lifted his head and spotted us. "Moon, you can go in. Coach is waiting for you."

Adam glanced at me. "What about Zeke?"

"He's with you."

He waved us on, but I walked up to him instead. "Thanks, Cam. I hope we can put everything behind us."

Cameron's gaze flicked to me. His fathomless eyes pinned me to the spot and probed me. "I already did, Manning. You and I are good. More importantly, we're done. There's no reason we should have anything to do with each other from now on."

I nodded, once, and then walked away. We understood each other completely. It was past time we went back to our own lives.

Adam and I got through security and went separate ways after the door. Adam joined Coach Nelson and the team in front of the locker room while I searched for a seat. I stopped scanning when I spotted Miss Val waving me over.

"Hello, Zeke. How are you?"

"I'm good." I shook hands with Mr. Shea as I sat down. "How's Jessie? When are you coming back?"

She beamed. "She's wonderful. Jessie is fawned over constantly by everyone in the house. She spends more time in our arms than in her crib and she loves the attention much like her father. I'll miss her when I come back next month, but I've got three hundred other kids who need me."

"We do. Your sub got rid of the candy and makes us do meditation exercises."

Her laughter rang out—soft and lovely like her. "I hope I'm liked for more than my candy."

"You definitely are... the candy just helps."

We collapsed into giggles until I realized what I was doing. I bit my lip, penning in my smile. I was resolved not to open up to Miss Val. Mom could make me go to therapy, but never again would I talk about that day. This would be easier if it wasn't so impossible not to like Val.

"Val, look," Ryder spoke up. "I think security has given them the all clear."

I strained over the heads to look. One of the security guys was speaking to Nelson. We watched them shake hands and then Nelson sent the boys in.

The tension leaked out of my shoulders. Cole and Adam would be fine.

"What a relief," said Val, echoing my thoughts. "This situation with the prankster has become serious. I almost didn't let Adam swim today."

I nodded. "This guy has been going after Elites, but I'm worried about all of them. We don't know why he's doing it to predict what will happen next."

"He?" Val shifted to face me, frowning slightly. "Are you using that pronoun in general?"

"No. We're convinced it must be a boy."

I explained our theory and got to hear her curse.

"Shit. Why didn't we see that? Of course, they couldn't risk being seen on the girls' campus," she cried. "I need to tell Mrs. Argyle—"

"Val? Val, look! There's something wrong!"

Our heads swung around to the scene below. Something was going on. Cole and the other Elite, Sullivan Porter, were out of the locker room. Both fully dressed, they spoke— no, argued with Coach by the wild gestures. Cole had something in his hand that he was waving in the guard's face.

"Excuse me!" Val and Ryder scurried off the bleachers and descended on the group.

My tension ratcheted up tenfold. What was going on? Where was Adam?

"Hello? Hello?" A voice came over the speakers. "Good afternoon, ladies and gentlemen. Please, bear with us for a few minutes. Everything is under control and we will begin soon."

I kept my attention fixed on Cole, so I witnessed the moment he threw the item down. My mouth fell open as Cole stormed out. Sullivan was two steps behind him.

What the hell happened?

The announcer came back on. "All right. The matter has been resolved and the meet will begin in twenty minutes. Thank you for your patience."

I pounced on Miss Val the second she came back. "What's going on? Why did Cole walk out? He'd sell vital organs before he'd miss this competition."

"He's been disqualified." There was a grim set to her lips. "The prankster, for lack of a better name, struck again."

"How? I thought security checked everything."

She shook her head. "They were smart. They switched out Cole and Sullivan's suits with ones that were identical in color and style, but not size. The guards didn't notice. These suits came down below the top of the kneecaps which is against regulation," she stated. "They're out of the meet. Coach Nelson is calling for their backup swimmers now."

"Did they... find a sticker?" It seemed a stupid question to ask, but I didn't know what else to say.

"They're searching again while the meet goes on, but this is no coincidence. After this, I will speak to the principal about what you told me. This has gone on long enough."

"COLE IS STILL ANGRY." I flipped onto my back and gazed up at the ceiling. "He won't talk about the meet. He walks away if I even mention it. Tomorrow is Michael's race and everyone is convinced he'll strike again. Lars Johansson is in the race too and he's threatened to drop out if the administration doesn't do something."

Derek dropped his head back. "How did this happen? One minute I was reading and the next you're in my room."

I swatted his foot. "Will you be serious? You're under attack, Derek."

He shrugged as he picked his book back up. "I told you to stop worrying about me. I'll be fine."

"How can you say that?" I propped myself up on my arm. "Do you know something I don't know?"

"No."

"Then you're talking out of your ass and therefore not reassuring me at all."

I spotted a grin before he lifted the book and blocked my view. "I played the Chesterfield/Breakbattle rematch and nothing happened."

"But the match was off campus."

"Exactly. So is the next one, and when we win, the match after that will be off campus too. The guy's not going off terrain and I'm safe in my room. I had maintenance upgrade my locks and no one is getting in here."

I let out a breath. All of that did make me feel better. "I just wish we knew why they were doing this."

"We do know."

I sat up fully at that. "What do you mean?"

"It's sabotage—plain and simple. Cole is pissed because members of the Elite Network were in the crowd. The kind that mark you for swimming scholarships and full rides down the line."

"They were? How do you know?"

He gave me a look.

"Oh. Right. Dumb question." I scooted up the bed and plucked the book from his fingers. "A better one is how would the prankster know that?"

"He wouldn't have to be in the Network to know important people come to our meets, competitions, and games. It's one of the reasons people send their kids to this place. But more than that, all he needs to know is how much Landon, Cole, Michael, Lars, and Sullivan wanted to win. If he's got a grudge against the Elites, he's found the best way to hit us where it hurts."

I slowly bobbed my head. "Then he will try something tomorrow."

"Probably, but I don't think this one will be easy," he said. "Michael and Lars don't keep their uniforms in the locker room or leave gym bags lying around. They'll be hard to get to and Whittaker's beefed up security."

Derek grabbed my arm and pulled me forward. I yelped when I suddenly found myself flying into the pillows.

"I'm trying to read," he said as I gaped at him. "Stop talking and read book one. If you like it, I'll let you borrow this when I'm done."

He tossed a book in my lap and went back to reading like it was no big deal. Seconds passed and then I did the same. Worrying wasn't going to help me figure out who the prankster was or what they were planning. I had to trust the staff were doing everything they could to catch him before he carried out those plans.

BEEP! BEEP! BEEP!

I groaned, burying deeper into the covers. What the hell was that noise?

Beep! Be—

The noise was brought to a blessed end and I relaxed, slipping back into sleep.

"What the fuck?!"

I jerked. Fright shot adrenaline into my bloodstream, ripping me awake, and for good this time. I turned around and scowled at the bleary smudge that was Derek. "You woke me up."

"I— You— What are you doing in my bed?!"

"I fell asleep."

"How?!"

I sat up and stretched as his pale face and bugged-out eyes came into focus. "You fell asleep first. I was reading the book you gave me and the next thing I knew I was out too. It's not a big deal." I squinted at the clock. "I'm starved. I'm going to get ready for breakfast. See you down there."

I grabbed the book and headed out, leaving him gaping after me. I cleaned up quickly and left for the cafeteria. Our table was mostly full by the time I went down. I turned to get my food and pulled up short.

Zach was in line with his girlfriend, Shannon. She was giggling over something he said and dropped kisses along his jaw.

Wow. It's against the rules for me to go into the library, but they're allowed to do that where we eat.

I hung back and let them go ahead. I didn't need a repeat of the last time I ran into those two.

"Where were you last night?" Adam asked when I finally sat down. It was just Owen, Justin, Adam, Nico, and Tanner this morning. Cole was sitting alone at a table near the head—no Michael in sight.

"I lost track of time." I changed the subject. "Have you seen Michael?"

He shook his head. "No. He's probably on the field."

That sounded right. I picked up my egg sandwich and dug in. I wanted to catch him before class to wish him luck.

Adam and I finished and stood at the same time. We walked out together, but he paused when I veered down the wrong hallway.

"Where are you going?"

"To find Michael."

"I'll come with."

We stepped out of the main building into the cool morning. I sucked in a deep lungful of air and let it out slowly. Part of me wished I hadn't missed our run this morning. This was the perfect time of day. The air cooled the sweat on your skin. The sun hadn't been up long enough to make the heat unbearable. Above all, was the peace. The quad was still and quiet.

"I spoke to Derek about the attacks," I began. "He thinks it's someone with a grudge out to make the Elite look bad, but I don't get how they've flown under the radar. Someone who hates them that much wouldn't be able to hide it, right?"

"Zeke," he whispered.

"I just don't understand how he's gotten around unnoticed and—"

Adam broke into a run. "Zeke! Get help!"

"What? What's going on?!" I sprinted after him. "Adam?!"

"Get the nurse! Now!"

Then I saw him.

Lying prone in the middle of the track, Michael didn't move at the sound of Adam's cries.

Derek lay at the foot of the boulder. His expression so perfect he could have been sleeping if not for the dark, growing pool beneath his head.

"Please! Don't leave!"

My feet tangled. I screamed as I was ripped free from the grip of my memories and hit the ground with a force that jarred my bones.

"Zeke, hurry!"

I didn't think of the pain. Scrambling to my feet, I spun around and raced for the main building, screaming for help the whole way.

Chapter Eight

"**S**porting events are canceled for the rest of the semester."

There were no groans. No shouts. No complaints. No one in the cafeteria spoke.

Whittaker stood before the head table. His eyes passed over the crowd as he addressed us.

"The attack on Mr. Foster and Mr. Young has turned this into a very different situation. What some may see as harmless pranks does not extend to drugging or physical harm. Both acts are punishable by expulsion from this academy and police involvement. The person responsible for these will be subjected to both. The time to step forward for a softer sentence has passed. We will be investigating these incidents and I will not rest until the responsible party is found."

I shivered as his gaze swept over our table. I had never seen this expression on Whittaker. Angry seemed too small a word to describe it.

"You are dismissed."

We rose and filed out of the room. We didn't break our silence until we reached the F Wing.

"This is bad," Tanner said. "Canceling sports?"

"They had no choice. Someone drugged Michael's water," said Adam. "He passed out mid-run and hit his head hard. When Lars heard, he refused to do the race and the other Elites started saying the same. They make up the majority of our best players. Why hold events if they refuse to show up?"

"This is so fucked up. This guy has covered his tracks so far. How are they going to find him?" He stopped before Dawson's door, blocking our way. "What happens if they don't?"

None of us had an answer for that, and as the weeks passed, it looked as though no one else did either.

Argyle and Whittaker brought students in for interviews. People traded guesses on what the upside-down A meant. We were on edge waiting for the next strike, but all I could do was get through school and be with my friends.

"I'm glad you came back, Landon." I folded my legs under me and got comfortable. We were supposed to be doing home-work, but somehow, we ended up on the couch and the television flicked on.

"Almost didn't. Henrietta and Declan wanted me to bask in all the privileges of being Elite. Being saddled with some psycho's grudge wasn't a part of the plan."

I rested my cheek against the cushion as I gazed at him. "What made them change their minds?"

"They left it up to me and I chose to come back. I like it here. I have friends here." His eyes met mine. No greens or jelly bean blues, but his natural brown—ordinary, common, beautiful. "I couldn't leave."

"Good," I whispered. "This place wouldn't be the same without you."

He adopted the same position, resting his cheek against the couch, and a lock of hair fell across his face.

As if it were the most natural thing in the world, I lifted my hand and pressed it to his forehead. My fingertips skated across his skin as I brushed his hair behind his ear. Then I looked into his eyes and reality crashed down around me.

I snatched my hand back. "I-I'm sorry! I didn't mean—"

"It's okay."

"No, I shouldn't have—"

"Hey." It wasn't his soft exclamation that silenced me. It was the smile that spread across his lips. "It's alright, Zeke."

A feeling I didn't know took hold of me. My skin tingled like a million fire ants were racing beneath the surface, and suddenly, I couldn't hold it in anymore.

Do it, Zela. Tell him who you are. Say, Landon, I'm a girl. I would have gone all four years without telling you, but denying how I feel is driving me crazy. I want to be with you.

I opened my mouth. "Landon—"

Landon's lips crashed down on mine.

"Mmrrph!"

My eyes popped. Reacting on surprise, I tried to pull away, but Landon's hand snaked around my waist. It pulled me closer while the other cupped the back of my neck.

What is happening?! What is happening?! What is—?!

Landon bit my lip. Just a playful nip, but it sent a surge of heat through me so intense my body spasmed.

The next thing I knew, my legs were wrapped around his waist while my fingers ran through his hair. Fire was the word to use to describe the feeling of being with Landon. I could feel my nerve endings come to life only to be burned away. Our tongues dueled in a furious battle that I was destined to lose.

Landon gripped my thighs and guided me onto my back. I went willingly, pulling him with me lest we break our kiss.

Knock. Knock.

I stilled.

Knock. Knock.

"Landon, it's Cole. Open up."

A bucket of ice water upended on my head—or it might as well have. I pulled away.

"Zeke, it's f-fine." His breath was labored. It ghosted over my lips enticing shivers from me. "He'll go away." Landon closed the distance between us.

Bang! Bang!

"Open up, man! I know Zeke is in there! I need him!"

The spell was broken. I scrambled away until the arm of the couch stopped me.

Landon groaned. "Give me a sec. I'll get rid of him."

I didn't say anything as he got up. I couldn't. Zeke had gotten his first kiss. Zeke who was really *Zela* had gotten his first kiss from Landon Foster!

What does this mean? Does Landon like Zeke?

Of course, he does, another voice snapped. *That's not how you kiss people you don't like!*

My eyes drifted to Landon as I pressed my fingers to my lips. But if Landon likes Zeke... does that mean he wouldn't want Zela?

"What do you want?" I heard him say.

"I need Zeke's help with a club assignment."

"Too bad. He's mine now."

I flushed hot.

"You'll have to wait your turn," said Landon.

"No, it's okay!"

Landon twisted around.

"I'll go," I said.

He gave me a put-out look that almost shattered my re-solve. "Why?"

Because I have never been happier or more confused in my life and the combination of the two is doing my head in.

"Because I need help on that assignment too." I shoved my shoes on and snatched up my things. "We'll hang out later."

Landon didn't move from the doorway and I was forced to duck under his arm.

"We'll finish what we were doing tomorrow."

I swallowed hard. "Yep," I rasped. "Tomorrow."

I didn't breathe again until I heard the door shut.

"Peterson's work is the last thing I have to do. Let's get it done." Cole squinted at me. "What's wrong with you? Are you sick? Why are you so red?"

"I'm fine. Let's go."

He shrugged and then turned to lead the way to his room. The hallway wasn't empty or quiet. Boys had their doors open and shouted at each other across the hall rather than change rooms. We passed by two guys huddled up in the doorway, laughing at something on their phone.

"What are you looking at, Rhys?"

The freckled boy grinned as he held out his phone. "Photos of your mom. May I say, she's still hot for her age."

Cole grabbed his phone with one hand and socked him square on the arm with the other.

"Ah!"

"Oh, shit," Cole breathed. "Who sent you this?"

"Blocked number, but it's getting passed around."

I rose up to peer over his shoulder. "See what?"

"This." Cole put the phone up to my face, giving me the full, unadulterated view of the penis.

"Argh!" I reeled back.

Rhys and the other guy burst out laughing. "No wonder Fields has such a complex," Rhys said.

Zach? That was a naked picture of Zach?

"I would be too if that was the equipment I was working with."

Cole shoved the phone at him. "Delete it now, and tell everyone else who has it to do the same."

Rhys shared a look with his friend that clearly said "who does this guy think he is?"

"Just having it on your phone is a two-week suspension, dumbass," Cole said. "Passing it around could get you expelled. Pretend like you getting in the Elite wasn't a fucking mistake and delete the picture."

Scowling, Rhys stalked off into a room across the hall. He slammed the door so hard the walls rattled.

"Idiot." Cole beckoned me on and kept on to his room. "I have nine more problems left. If we finish quick, you can go back to whatever you were doing with Landon."

There was a strong chance I would be red for the rest of the night.

"There's no rush."

THE NEXT DAY, MY HEAD was in a fog. Landon kissed me. He kissed me.

That fact, and every single detail surrounding it, repeated in my mind on a loop. What was I supposed to do? Jordan joked about it, but I never considered the possibility of a boyfriend. What did any of that matter when I was here for Derek? But then I met these guys and fell for them when I wasn't paying attention. Secretly crushing was one thing, but I couldn't go to the next level with Landon as Zeke. I had to tell him the truth.

Maybe I'm getting ahead of myself. What if he doesn't want to go to the next level? The kiss could have been a one-time thing.

And my spiral continued.

"Zeke? Zeke?"

I shook myself. "What's up?"

"Breakfast. You coming?'

"No, I'm not hungry. You go ahead."

"Want me to bring you back something?"

"I'll take an apple or some fruit."

"Alright. See ya."

I stretched out on my bed after Adam left and traced the mystery stains on the ceiling. Crushes were never supposed to happen, but they did. I could be friends with Landon and hide who I was, but I couldn't kiss him and lie to him. I had to tell him the truth.

But what if he reveals my secret and I get kicked over to the girls' side. It's not about getting Derek's trust anymore. It's about keeping it. He would never forgive me if he found out.

I groaned. Why did I do this? Every time I made up my mind, I thought of a reason I should go the other way.

If only someone could choose for me.

A knock sounded at the door.

Oh my... Landon?

His name didn't have a chance to fully penetrate my mind before I was up and across the room. I took a steadying breath as I closed my hand over the knob.

Okay. I've made up my mind. I'm telling him the truth.

I threw open the door.

"Mr. Manning."

My smile evaporated at the sight of Principal Whittaker and the two men flanking him on either side. "Yes, sir."

"Mr. Manning, I need you to step outside so these gentlemen can search your room."

I blinked. "Excuse me?"

He looked me in the eyes, no trace of the charming smile to be seen. "A student has come forward anonymously and revealed that you were behind the attacks on the Elite Class. I have reason to believe you are the upside-down A."

There is a moment, right before you throw up, when it all wells up inside of you. You feel your stomach rebel, your throat clench, your breath stop, and it's a horrible feeling for the fact that you know the worst is coming and there's nothing you can do to stop it.

"An anonymous student?" I forced out. "That's not possible. No one could have said that because it's not true. I'm not behind the attacks."

Whittaker's expression didn't change. "Step outside, Mr. Manning."

"But you can't just search my room without—"

"Student domiciles are subject to search if and when the faculty have reason to believe the student has committed an infraction against the policies of the academy," he rattled off. "Outside. Now."

I hesitated only a moment longer before stepping out. The security guys streamed in.

"Stand in this doorway. Do not move."

I nodded. Whittaker walked inside and went straight for my backpack. I balled my fists as he unzipped it and tossed the contents out on the bed.

"Zeke?"

Goodness. How is that for timing?

Landon strode down our unimpressive hallway looking out of place not because of the E, but the mere fact that he was the most gorgeous thing that would walk these carpets.

"Adam told me to bring you this." He held up an apple.

"Did he?"

He shrugged. "I may have offered."

I tensed as he drew near.

"What's going on in there?"

"Someone is playing a messed-up game. The attacker—"

"Oh, you heard about that." Landon took my hand and gently turned my wrist. He placed the apple on my palm and I shivered as his fingers skated over mine. "They got Zach."

"Got Zach?"

"They stole his girlfriend's phone and sent pics of him to all of the Elites."

"That's awful," I said. "I don't like him, but that's too far."

I glanced inside my room where they were now stripping my bed.

"I get why he skipped out on the cafeteria, but what about you?"

I lowered my gaze to our clasped hands. "I wasn't hungry. I thought I'd take some time to think."

"Think about what?"

"About the best time to tell the truth," I whispered.

"The answer to that is always sooner rather than later."

He took a step closer and the smell of him filled my lungs. In the next breath, I was transported to last night. His sweet scent engulfing me, his hands burning my skin, and his lips making me feel things I never had before.

I liked him. Telling him the truth might sink us before we start, but he was right. It was better he know now.

"I want to talk to you," I began, "and tell you the truth about me. I just need to deal with this first. Can we meet up in your room tonight?"

"Sure." He squeezed my fingers. "We didn't finish up last night anyway."

I ducked my head as my face warmed. Last night was the first time I had ever done anything with a guy. I wasn't on the level of casual innuendoes yet.

"Mr. Manning? Explain this, please."

"Explain what, sir?" I looked up and my mouth fell open. My mattress pad was destroyed. The lining that separated the memory foam topper had been slashed open. "Sir?! Why did you do that?"

"It is you who needs to explain yourself." He stuck his hand inside the pad. I watched in confusion as he opened his palm. "And you will do so in my office. Now."

"Zeke?" Landon breathed. "What the hell is this?"

I choked. "I-I've never seen that before."

"Oh my—" He dropped my hand as he backed away. "That's what you wanted to tell me, isn't it? You were behind the attacks."

"No. Those stickers aren't mine!"

He staggered back. "You were playing me? You messed with my contacts?" He gazed at me with such hurt it twisted my stomach. "Why? To get back at me for going with Cameron? For all the battles? Why?!"

I jumped. "Landon, please, listen to me. I didn't do this. I would never hurt you or anyone else. You're my... friend."

For the barest moment, uncertainty flickered across his face.

Whittaker stepped out of my ransacked dorm. "We have a witness that saw you switch out Mr Porter's and Mr. Reed's uniforms for the pair that got them disqualified. There will be no using that excuse to escape punishment."

Landon's face shuttered closed. He stormed out amid my shouts for him to come back.

"I DIDN'T DO THIS."

"You were seen."

"By who?!" I placed my hand over my stomach, willing it to ease. "Tell me who supposedly saw me switch the suits."

"The student will remain anonymous."

"The student is a liar."

"That is enough, Manning."

"But you can't do this to me on the word of one person."

"It's not due to one word. It's because of this." He pointed to the pile of stickers on his desk. The hundreds of tiny little upturned As that were sewn into my mattress pad.

My throat tightened. It was so hard to swallow.

"I'm being framed, sir. I would never do this."

He leaned back in his seat. "Never? You wouldn't get back at the people who caused you to miss the placement test. You wouldn't be angry at those who battled you over and over again, taking what you had even though they have everything." He picked up a sticker and held it up. "I'm told that this is a math symbol that means for all. Did you think you were striking back for everyone outside of the Elite Class?"

"I did not do this!" I cried.

"I don't believe you," he said calmly. "Zeke Manning, you are expelled from Breakbattle Academy."

Whittaker might have said more, but I could hear nothing for the roaring that filled my ears. My nails dug into my stomach. Landon's face as he walked away. That palmful of stickers. A faceless enemy plotting against me. Expulsion from Breakbattle Academy and... Derek.

It was all too much. I couldn't breathe. I couldn't think. I couldn't—

"It's me. Wait for me!"

I toppled out of my chair and heaved.

"IT'S GOING TO BE OKAY, Mr. Manning. Gillian will get it all cleaned up. There's no need to cry." I felt a tentative pat on my head. "It's an unfortunate part of my job, but I have to make the hard decisions," said Whittaker. "I can't ignore the evidence against you."

I wailed louder.

"Heaven's sake— Dewan? Dewan!"

The door banged open. "Yes, sir?"

"Get Miss Moon. Now!"

My chest heaved with wracking sobs. I didn't come this far and do all the things I did to lose it now. I'm happy here. I'm making friends. Derek hadn't let me all the way in, but he's cracked open the door. I couldn't go. I had to convince Whittaker I was being set up.

I opened my mouth, but only more sobs poured out.

"Hello? Zeke?" Val cried. "What's the matter?" The chaise dipped and then arms encircled me. "Principal Whittaker?"

"Zeke has just been informed he no longer attends Breakbattle Academy. Mr. Manning is responsible for the attacks against the Elite students."

"It wasn't me," I protested from the circle of her arms. "You have to believe me, Miss Val. I was set up."

"You must have been because the idea that you're behind this is ridiculous."

My tears came to a hiccupping halt. What did she say?

"There's no way Zeke drugged Michael Young, messed with Landon Foster's contact solution, or sent around nude photos."

"I've brought students in over the weeks and questioned them on who could have a grudge against the Elites and Mr. Manning's name came up more than once," Whittaker replied. "He began the year in multiple battles with them, most that he lost.

"He decided to get back at them and not only was he witnessed carrying out one of his deeds, but the attacker's calling card was found in his mattress pad. That cannot easily be explained away."

"Yes, it can."

"Yes, it—? Miss Moon, have you heard a word that I've said?" Temper was snaking into his voice. "Cruel, dangerous attacks were carried out on our students. This must be taken seriously."

"I agree. It's a very serious situation if the student responsible for these attacks have set up another to be blamed for it. You said the stickers were found in the mattress pad, but I get the battle reports. For a good part of the year, the mattress pad has not been in Zeke's possession."

My sobs ceased. I jerked my head up and stared at Miss Val as that statement burrowed into my skull.

"That is true, but—"

"Those stickers could have been planted at any time during the weeks it was out of his sight," Miss Val said.

"That's right," I whispered, "and the only reason they had my pad and all of my things is because..."

Cameron ordered them to take it from me.

My nails dug painfully into my palms. How did I not see it? It wasn't over. It had never been over.

"I was set up from the very beginning." My voice sounded odd to my own ears—dull, lifeless. "Create a reason for me to have a grudge against the Elites with constant battles. Every loss looked bad for me and gave him plenty of options to plant the evidence. He only had to wait for me to win it back and return it to my room.

"Then a series of attacks that were harsher on the boys who battled me and when the time was right, a *witness* comes forward to blame it all on me. The perfect plan to see me out of Breakbattle Academy forever."

A profound silence followed my final word. Gillian stopped scrubbing to join the others in staring at me.

"Who are you talking about, Zeke?" Val asked.

His name burned my tongue. "Cameron Dupre."

Whittaker held up a hand. "Hold on. You can't make accusations like that without proof. Mr. Dupre is one of our tops students who—"

"Who was given detention for two months because of his part in an awful prank against the new students," Miss Val finished. "He may be behind this, or it could be someone else, but no action should be taken until we've exhausted all avenues.

"We received a lot of criticism for allowing personal items to be subject to the battle system, but if it's discovered the rule change led to a crafty student having the perfect opportunity to frame and expel a student, this will harm our reputation and the plans for expansion."

I fixed on Whittaker. As usual, his expression gave nothing away, but there was a vein jumping in his forehead that said he might not be as unaffected as he appeared. Seconds passed and Gillian did not resume her cleaning.

"Very well," he stated. "The expulsion is rescinded."

My breath whooshed out of me. "Thank you, sir."

"Until such a time as I've investigated your claims and how many people had access to your mattress pad. Miss Moon, you can help me reinterview the classes, as well as the anonymous student."

"I'm happy to help." She patted my back as she stood, communicating for me to come with her. "I won't stand for our students to be messed around. We'll get to the truth of this."

Whittaker's eyes met mine. "That we will."

I thanked him once more as Miss Val led me from the office. "Thank you, Miss Val. I can't believe what almost happened."

"I know it wasn't you, Zeke," she said softly. She walked us away from Dewan and out into the hall. "You're too good a person to have done those things, but you have clearly upset someone for them to go to these lengths. I'm going to get to the bottom of this and make sure the right person is held responsible. In the meantime, I want you to keep your head down and your eyes open. Don't let on that we believe you were set up. Let them think they're safe."

"Okay, I will." School would be over in a couple of weeks. I could keep quiet for that long.

"Go on to class. I promise this will be over soon."

Her reassurance buoyed me as I left the main building. She believed me even if Whittaker was on the fence. She wouldn't stand by and let me be expelled which Cameron never accounted for in his plan.

I walked in just as Coach Nelson blew his whistle. "Final block, you're up."

"Sorry I'm late, Coach."

"I was told you would be," he replied. "No tardy. Just get changed and focus up. You're practicing a new stroke today."

Class was actually fun today. Tanner and I learned the breaststroke pretty quickly and then spent the rest of the time trying it out and messing around.

Coach's whistle brought our fun to an end. "Alright. Out of the water and get changed."

The boys clambered out of the pool and led a dripping march to the locker room. I grabbed a seat on the bleachers while I waited for them to finish.

One after the other, the guys emerged from the locker room fresh and dry from their shower. Tanner was the last one out.

"Meet up in my dorm after," he called. "I've got your assignments."

"Okay."

Tanner slipped out the door as another student came in.

"Coach Nelson," said Lars. "Can I talk to you? It's about moving to the expert block."

"Let's take this to my office."

The two walked off to the door on the other side of the pool while I hurried to the locker room. Having to wait while everyone else showered meant I was chilled through by the time I had my turn. All I wanted was to wash away the chlorine under a steaming hot spray.

I crossed to my locker and opened it. Out came my towel, shampoo, and moisturizing scrub.

Eeek.

"I'm in here," I called as the door creaked open. "I'm still dressed. You can come in."

"We were going to do that anyway."

Zach?

The name had no sooner crossed my mind before a rough hand gripped my arm. He yanked me around and slammed me into the locker. Pain exploded in my head as it collided with the metal.

"What are you doing?!"

"We know it was you!"

I blinked, vision clearing as I saw who *we* was. Rhys, Sullivan, Wyatt, Jose, Cole, Michael, and Landon fanned out around me, blocking me on all sides.

"What is this?" I yanked out of Zach's grasp. "Why are you here?"

Cole bared his teeth. "Are you fucking serious? Landon told us everything. We know you sabotaged us!"

"That wasn't me! I was framed!"

"Like fuck!" Zach punched the locker, inches from my head. "You sent those pictures to everyone because I took your precious shit! It wasn't enough that you turned my friends against me!"

"I didn't—"

"You never forgave us for going along with Cameron's orders. You've been out to humiliate us from the start." Fury glittered in Cole's eyes as his fists balled. "There were scouts at the meet, but you made sure they only saw Moon! I told you how much I wanted that win and you took it away!"

"Look at what you did to me," Michael hissed. The white bandage shown starkly against his forehead, but it didn't cover the healing marks from his face scraping against the unforgiving track. "I tried to help you."

"Michael, no—"

"And you played me," Landon whispered. "Was it all an act, Zeke?"

I had seen many expressions on Landon's face, but never this one. The coldness in his eyes made my stomach heave. How could he look at me like that? How could they think I would do these things?

"It wasn't an act, Landon." I looked deep in his eyes. "It was real for me. I did forgive you—all of you—and I would never do anything to hurt you. You have to believe me. I'm being set up."

Something flickered within those warm brown pools and my hope soared.

"No."

My head snapped to Cole.

"No," he repeated. "We're not falling for your bullshit anymore. You sabotaged me and Sullivan for Moon. You got close to Michael and learned his routine and when to spike his water bottle. You made Landon train you so you could get close to his gym bag. Now that we know, it all makes sense. This is what you do. You made your little plan to get back at Cameron, and now you've gotten all of us."

The wetsuit blanketed me in the pool water, making the chill seep into every part of my body, but that wasn't why I trembled.

"I didn't do this, Cole. There is someone who would want to frame me and I'm sure you know who it is. Don't play into his hand."

Michael shook his head. "We're not the ones being fooled. You've been fooled because you thought we were nice guys who'd take your shit lying down."

Landon's voice was low and steady. "Show him he's wrong, boys."

"Wha—" Zach seized me. "No!" I screamed as I was thrown into the waiting arms of the Elites. Sullivan and Rhys caught me and twisted my arms around my back.

"Stop! Hel—"

Zach buried his fist in my gut, punching the air out of me. I gasped, doubling over, and they let me fall to the floor. The cold tile stung my cheek as I clutched my stomach. I didn't get a chance to catch my breath before the blows rained down. I curled tight into a ball, tears leaking from my eyes, as they kicked, punched, and tore at me.

Cole, Michael, and Landon just stood there the whole time, watching them break me.

"That's enough," Landon eventually spoke up.

"What?" Zach cried. His shoe was buried in my back. "Why?"

"We have to get out before Nelson comes back. Go!"

Hands released me and the blurred figures faded as I heard the door open and shut.

"I said leave, Fields."

"No, I'm not letting him off after he showed my dick to the whole fucking school! He thinks that shit is funny, then let's see how he likes it."

My eyes widened as I realized what that meant. I started screaming before he grabbed me.

"No! Get off!" I swung blindly and connected.

"Ah!" Zach flew back, clutching his nose, and I tried to scramble away.

"Stop, Zach!" Michael shouted. "That's enough!"

"I'll say when it's enough! This little shit stole my friends and humiliated me!"

Zach grabbed my ankle in a grip like iron. I kicked and bucked as he dragged me back, and then climbed on top of me, pinning me down. His hand closed over the zipper.

"No!" The scream tore from my hoarse throat. "Help me! Someone help!"

"Get off him, Zach!"

Cole, Michael, and Landon tackled him from behind. They grabbed him around the arms and neck and pulled. Zach went flying back, but he did not release his hold. My zipper ripped down to below my bindings before his fingers slipped off.

My bare feet scrabbled against the tile as I flipped over, desperately trying to hide.

"Let me goooo!" I heard a grunt and someone cry out.

I shrieked when something clamped down on my neck. Zach ripped the wetsuit all the way off. Cool air smacked my backside as it was exposed to their eyes. Zach's nails dug into the soft flesh of my thigh and I was flipped over.

"What the... fuck..."

"He's a girl?" Zach scrambled off me. "He's a girl!"

"Oh no," someone breathed. "What did we do?"

Uncontrollable sobs wracked my body. I couldn't see their faces through the tears, but they could see me—all of me.

"Zeke?! Zeke!" His voice broke through, reaching me before the door slammed open. "Zeke! Where is he?! What did you do?!"

"I-I didn't know!" Zach shrieked. "Derek, I swear I didn't know!"

"What the fuck are you talking—"

I curled my knees tight to my chest, sobs growing louder. *He's seen. He knows. It's all over.*

"Get out. All of you. Now!"

I heard the squeaks of rubber soles retreating, and then ones coming toward me. My eyes flew open when something was draped over my body.

Derek wrapped me tight in the towel. "It's going to be okay, Zeke." He lifted me onto his lap and secured me to his chest. "I'm sorry I wasn't here sooner. I promise they'll never touch you again."

Derek repeated that to me over and over again as I buried my nose in his chest and cried.

"ZEKE?"

I folded my blazer and placed it in my suitcase. "You can call me Zela, Adam. We're alone."

"Right. Sorry."

Zela. It was still odd hearing my name within these walls.

After Derek came for me, he carried me up to his room and called for Adam. The shock knocked Adam sideways for a moment, but he put it aside when he saw the shape I was in. My lips split, right eyes swelling shut, and purpling bruises covering my body. The two of them cleaned me up, took care of me, and Derek let me sleep in his bed that night. Not once did they ask me why, and I didn't offer an explanation. Our final weeks of school passed in an uneasy silence until it was finally time to leave.

Adam's things were already packed and by the door. He sat on the edge of his stripped mattress and watched me.

"Do you want to talk about it?" he asked.

I didn't pause in my packing. "Not right now."

"Listen... you're my best friend. Nothing will change that."

Tears prickled at the back of my eyes. "I know," I whispered. "Thank you. That means a lot."

"You're going to come over this summer, right? Hang by the pool. Play with Jessie. Watch movies. Get kicked around by Esme."

Despite myself, a tiny laugh escaped my lips. "Yeah. I can't miss out on that."

"Good. And when we come back next year, things are going to be different."

"I agree."

I shifted around, turning my back to Adam as I pretended to repack something.

Things are going to be very different next year. They thought I was coming for them before, they'll know what it's like when I do it for real. Forget Zela and Zeke, someone else entirely would be coming back to Breakbattle next year... and the Elites better watch out.

If you'd like to read the next book in the series, The Execution, click here.[1]

The Execution

They think they won.

The Elite thought it would end at the battle, but I'm taking them to war.

I will topple Landon, Michael, and Cole off their thrones even if it means bringing the system to its knees.

Tensions are boiling beneath the surface of Breakbattle Academy. Protests are erupting, the lower classes are fighting back, and the Elites aren't as invulnerable as they thought. The school is ready to blow.

All they need is the right girl to light the match.

Keep In Touch

Join Ruby's mailing list for news, teasers, and more:
https://www.subscribepage.com/rubyvincentpage
Join Ruby's Facebook Reader Group:
https://bit.ly/3bNuCOq

ABOUT THE AUTHOR

Ruby Vincent is a published author with many novels under her belt but now she's taking a fun foray into contemporary romance. She loves saucy heroines, bold alpha males, and weaving a tale where both get their happy ever after.

www.ingramcontent.com/pod-product-compliance
Lightning Source LLC
Chambersburg PA
CBHW032031310726
48972CB00002B/631